THE ATOM STATION

Halldór Laxness (1902–98) was born near Reykjavík, Iceland. His first novel was published when he was seventeen. The undisputed master of contemporary Icelandic fiction and one of the outstanding novelists of the twentieth century, he wrote more than sixty books and his work has been translated into thirty languages. He was awarded the Nobel Prize for Literature in 1955.

Magnus Magnusson is an Icelander who was brought up in Scotland. Although justly celebrated for his achievements as a television presenter and his journalism, he is also the translator of several volumes of classical Icelandic sagas and modern novels, including Laxness's *The Fish Can Sing*. He was awarded an honorary knighthood (KBE) in 1989.

ALSO BY HALLDÓR LAXNESS

Independent People
The Fish Can Sing

Halldór Laxness

THE ATOM STATION

TRANSLATED FROM THE ICELANDIC BY
Magnus Magnusson

Random House Australia (Pty) Limited
20 Alfred Street, Milsons Point, Sydney,
New South Wales 2061, Australia

Random House New Zealand Limited
18 Poland Road, Glenfield,
Auckland 10, New Zealand

Random House (Pty) Limited
Endulini, 5A Jubilee Road, Parktown 2193,
South Africa

Random House Group Limited Reg. No. 954009
www.randomhouse.co.uk

A CIP catalogue record for this book
is available from the British Library

VINTAGE

Published by Vintage 2004

2 4 6 8 10 9 7 5 3 1

Copyright © Helgafell, 1948
English translation © Methuen & Co. Ltd., 1961, 2003

First published with the title *Atómstöðin* by
Helgafell, Reykjavík, 1948

First published in Great Britain in 1961 by
Methuen & Co. Ltd

Revised edition published in 2003 by
The Harvill Press

Vintage
Random House, 20 Vauxhall Bridge Road,
London SW1V 2SA

ISBN 0 09 945515 3

Papers used by Random House are natural, recyclable
products made from wood grown in sustainable forests.
The manufacturing processes conform to the environ-
mental regulations of the country of origin

Printed and bound in Denmark by
Nørhaven Paperback, Viborg

Contents

NOTE ON PRONUNCIATION

The only extra consonants in Icelandic used in this translation are:

ð(Ð), the so-called "crossed d" or "eth", which is pronounced like the voiced *the* in *breathe*
and
Þ (þ) which is pronounced as the unvoiced *th* in *thin*

The pronunciation of the vowels is conditioned by the same accents:

á as in *owl*
é as in *ye*, in *yet*
í as in *seen*
ó as in *note*
ö as in French *fleur*
ú as in *moon*
ý as in *seen*
æ as in *life*
au as in French *oeil*
ei, as in y in *tray*

1

BUDÚBÓDÍ

"Am I to take in this soup?" I ask.

"Yes, in the name of Jesus," says the dull-eared house-keeper, one of the greatest female sinners of our time; she had a glossy picture of the Saviour hanging up over the stainless steel sink. The younger daughter of the house, a six-year-old mite named Þórgunnur, but called Dídí, never leaves her side, stares at her with the fear of God in her eyes (and sometimes with clasped hands), eats with her in the kitchen, and sleeps with her at night; and from time to time the child looks censoriously, almost accusingly, at me, the new maid.

I summoned up my courage and went into the dining room with the soup tureen. The family was not yet at the table. The elder daughter, newly confirmed, came in looking as fresh-coloured as cream except for her black-painted lips and nails, adjusting with supple fingers her thick, blonde, cork-screw curls. I said Good evening, but she looked at me distantly, sat down at the table, and went on reading a fashion magazine.

Then the lady of the house comes bustling in with brisk, short steps, giving off a chilly breath of perfume; not really a fat woman, but plump and sleek and satisfied, her bracelets jingling. She does not look at me, exactly, but says as she seats herself, "Well, my dear, have you learned to use the electric floor-polisher yet? That's our Dúdú there," pointing to her daughter, "and here comes my Bóbó. And then we have a bigger one who's now in his first year at university – he's out enjoying himself tonight."

"How is an innocent girl from the north to memorise these barbarian names?" I hear someone say behind me. It is a tall, slim man with a Roman nose and a fine head, just starting to go grey at the temples. He takes off his horn-rimmed spectacles and begins to polish them; his smile, although unrestrained, is at the same time a little tired and absent. So this is the Member of Parliament for our constituency up in the north, the man in whose house I am now in service: Búi Árland, business magnate and Doctor of Philosophy.

When he has polished his spectacles and looked at me long enough he offers me his hand and says, "It was good of you to come all the way from the north to help us here in the south."

And by that time I had begun to get palpitations; and was sweating; and could not say a word, of course.

He murmurs my name to himself: "Ugla – owl," and then goes on, "A learned bird, and her time is the night. But how is my old friend Falur of Eystridalur with his herd of wild horses? And the church? I hope we shall manage to squeeze some money out of this utterly heathenish Parliament next session so that the winds can sing psalms out there in the valley when everything is laid waste. But the wild horses will have to look after themselves in their own divine way, because the German horse-dealers are now *kaput*."

How relieved I was that he should carry on talking, to give me time to pull myself together, for this was the first time that talking to a man had ever made me feel funny in the knees. I said that I was going to learn to play the church harmonium, and that this was the main reason I had come south: "We do not want the valley to be laid waste."

I had not had time to take notice of the chubby, overweight Bóbó staring at me as I talked to his father while Madam ladled out the soup, until now he suddenly gave a roar of laughter, bulged his cheeks until they could hold no more air, and exploded. His sister stopped leafing through the English fashion magazine and burst out laughing, too. In the open doorway to the kitchen behind me stands little angel-face, with no fear of God in her now, laughing and saying to her foster-mother in explanation of this unusual family hilarity, "She's going to learn to play the harmonium!"

Madam smiled to herself as she glanced at them, but their father gestured at them with his left hand and shook his head and kept his eyes fixed on my face, all at the same time, but said nothing and started to take his soup.

It was not until I had become used to seeing the elder daughter seat herself at the grand piano and dash off some Chopin impromptu as if nothing could be more natural, that I realised how ludicrous it was to hear a big, strapping north-country girl announce in a civilised home that she was going to learn to play the harmonium.

"That's just like you northerners, to start talking to people," said the cook when I returned to the kitchen.

Rebellion stirred in me and I replied, "I am people."

My trunk had already been moved in, as well as my harmonium. I had bought the latter that same day with all the money I had ever owned in my life, and it had still not been enough. My room was on the attic floor, two storeys up; I was allowed to practise whenever I had the time, except when there were visitors. My job was to keep the house clean, get the children off to school, help the cook-housekeeper and serve at table. The house was much more perfect than the sort of gilt-bordered Christmas-card Heaven which a crooked-nosed woman would sacrifice everything to attain in the next world: it was an all-electric house, with machines being plugged in and started up all day long; there was no such thing as a fire; heat came from hot springs underground, and the glowing embers in the fireplace were made of glass.

When I took in the main course the laughter had subsided; the young girl had begun to talk to her father, and only the little fat one was gazing at me. Madam said that she and her husband were "going out", whatever that involved, and that Jóna, the cook, was going to a meeting. "You are to look after the house and wait up for Bubu with something hot."

"Bu . . . pardon?" I said.

"Yet another barbarian," said the master of the house. "Apparently from Tanganyika, or Kenya; or the land where they decorate their hair with rats' tails. That aside, the boy is called Arngrímur."

"My husband isn't very *chic*," said Madam. "He would prefer to call the boy Grímsi. But modern times are *chic*. Everything has to be *à la mode*."

Her husband said, "You are from the north, from that unforgettable valley of Eystridalur, the daughter of Wild-horses Falur who is building a church: won't you please re-christen the children for me?"

"I would rather be chopped up into a hundred thousand million pieces than be called Gunsa," said the elder daughter.

"Her name, in fact, is Guðný," said her father. "But they cannot get by with less than Africa at its very darkest – bu-bu, dú-dú, bó-bó, dí-dí . . ."

At that, the woman looked hard at her husband and said, "Is that the way you're going to talk to the maid?" And to me: "Clear the dishes and take them to the kitchen, my girl."

NOT AFRAID OF HER

But I was not afraid of her at all, nor was I when I went in to her bedroom with her shiny silver shoes (my own flatties had been bought in the village of Sauðárkrókur). She was sitting very scantily clad before a large mirror with another mirror at an angle behind her, painting her toenails and humming. Undressed, she was fatter than I had thought, but nowhere flabby.

When I had laid down her shoes and was on my way out again she stopped humming, saw me behind her in the mirror, and said, with her back towards me, "How old are you, by the way?"

I told her – twenty-one.

"Are you quite uneducated?" she asked.

"Yes," I replied.

"And never been away from home before?"

"I had a year at domestic college in the north."

She turned round on the seat and looked directly at me. "At domestic college?" she echoed. "What did you learn there?"

"Oh, nothing, more or less," I said.

She looked at me and said, "You have a faintly educated look about you. An educated girl never has an educated look. I cannot stand an educated look on women. It's Communism. Look at me, I passed my university entrance, but I don't show it. Girls should be feminine. May I see your hair, my dear?"

I went over to her and she examined my hair, and I asked if she thought I had a wig, or perhaps lice.

She cleared her throat haughtily, and said as she pushed me from her, "Remember where you are."

I was going to leave the room without a word, but she saw my crestfallen look and said, to console me, "You have strong hair, but it's a muddy yellow. It could wash better."

I told her the truth, that I had washed it the day before yesterday, before I left home.

"In cow's urine?" she asked.

"Soft-soap," I replied.

She said, "You could wash it better, I say."

When I was halfway out of the door she called me back again and said, "What opinions do you hold?"

"Opinions? Me? None."

"All right, my girl, that's fine," she said. "And not one of those who wallow in books, I hope?"

"I have lain awake many a night with a book."

"God in Heaven help you," the woman said, and looked at me aghast. "What were you reading?"

"Everything."

"Everything?"

"In the country, everything is read," I said, "beginning with the Icelandic sagas; and then everything."

"But not the Communist paper, surely?" she said.

"We read whatever papers we can get for nothing out in the country," I replied.

"Take care not to become a Communist," said Madam. "I knew a lower-class girl once who read everything and became a Communist; she landed up in one of those cells."

"I'm going to be an organist," I said.

"Yes, you certainly come from the depths of the country," said the woman. "Off you go now, my dear."

No, I was not in the least afraid of her, even though she was closely related to the Government and I the daughter of old Falur in the north, who was trying to build a roof over God's head but whose horses went roofless all the year round; and she made of porcelain, I of clay.

2

THIS HOUSE – AND OUR FARM

The cook said she had been in many faiths, but had at last found a haven in the one which preached the true Christianity. This faith had been discovered in Småland and was financed by the Swedes, but had emigrated across the Atlantic and was now called after an American city with a long name which I cannot remember. She wanted me to come with her to a meeting. She said she had never received full forgiveness for her sins until she joined this Småland-American group.

"What sins are they?" I asked.

"I was a simply terrible person," she said. "But pastor Domselíus says that I can hop after two years."

According to the Småland-American faith people started hopping, as it were, when they became holy. But sins so burdened this big-boned woman that she had difficulty in rising off the ground. When I said that I had no sins she looked at

me with pity and dismay but offered to pray for me nevertheless and claimed that this would help, for she reckoned that
the god of the Småland-American group paid special regard
to her and followed her advice. She had been forbidden to
take the child Dídí with her to evening meetings, but before
she went out she would drag the poor thing out of bed and
make her kneel on the floor for a long time in her spotted
nightdress, hands clasped under her chin, and recite fearful
litanies to Jesus, confessing to countless crimes and beseeching
the Saviour not to take vengeance on her, until eventually the
tears would be streaming down the child's cheeks.

All life abandoned the house in the evening, and I was left
alone in this new world which in a single day had made my
previous life a dim memory – I am tempted to say a story in
an old book. There were three reception rooms, forming an
L-shape, crammed full of treasures. These thousand lovely
objects seemed to have made their way there of their own
accord, without any effort, as livestock make for an unfenced
meadow in the growing season. Here there was not one chair
so cheap that it could be bartered for our autumn milch cow;
and all our sheep would not fetch nearly enough to seat this
whole family at once. I am sure that the carpet in the big
drawing room cost more than our farm, even including all the
buildings. We only owned one article of furniture, the sagging
divan which my father bought in an auction some years ago,
and only the one picture, a portrait of Picture-Grímur, as we
children used to call old Hallgrímur Pétursson*, in his pulpit
surrounded by his holy pictures; and also, of course, the old
harmonium, my dream, but that had been out of order, alas,
for as long as I could remember, because there was no stove
in the room. The wild horses were our only luxury. Why do
those who labour never own anything? Or was I a Communist
to ask such a question, the ugliest of all ugliness, the only thing
one had to take care to avoid? I fingered a note on the piano

*Iceland's most celebrated and best-loved hymn-writer (1614–74).

in the house – and what a paradise of tone if it were played in harmony! If there is such a thing as sin, then it is a sin not to be able to play a musical instrument; and yet I had told the old woman that I had no sins. But the worst was when I went into the master's study near the front door, nothing but books from floor to ceiling – no matter where my hand paused, I could not understand a word. If there is any such thing as crime, then it is a crime to be uneducated.

CORPSE IN THE NIGHT

Finally I went up to my room and played on my new harmonium the two or three tunes I knew from the north, as well as the tune which only those who know nothing know: it is played with crossed hands. I was disgusted at myself for being so uneducated, and took out one of those dreary educational books published by *Mál og Menning** which eventually, one hopes, would make something of anyone who could be bothered to read them.

Thus the evening passed, and the people began to straggle home one by one; first the cook from the Småland-American absolution business, then the middle children, separately, and finally the master and mistress; soon everything was quiet. But the one I was waiting up for with hot food in the oven did not come and then it was 3 a.m., with me wandering about the house to keep myself awake, until at last I dropped off in one of those deep armchairs downstairs. At about 4 a.m. the doorbell rang, and I went to the door heavy-eyed with sleep and opened it. There were two policemen standing there, carrying between them a horizontal figure. They bade me Good evening, formally, and asked if I lived there and whether they could just dump a small corpse in the hall.

"That depends," I replied. "Whose is the corpse?"

---

*'Iceland's leading literary publisher, literally "Language and Culture".

They said that I would find out soon enough, tossed the corpse on to the floor, saluted, said Good night as formally as they had made their greeting, started up their car, and were gone; and I closed the door.

The man lay on the floor, if you could call him a man; he was more or less just at the shaving stage, his hair still bright with childhood, and he had his father's head. His coat and new shoes were covered with mud, as was one of his cheeks, as if he had fallen asleep in a puddle or had been rolled through a swamp; and there was vomit down his front. What was I to do? When I bent over him I heard him breathe. In addition to the stink of vomit, he reeked of poison – tobacco and schnapps. Luckily I had sometimes seen men paralysed by Black Death* at public festivities out in the country, so I knew what was up, and decided to try to bundle him up to his room on my own rather than rouse such splendid and cultivated parents – and they the owners of this wonderful house, too, more perfect than Heaven. I shook him lightly but he only moaned a little, and his eyes did not open except for a thin glimpse of white between his eyelids. I soaked a sponge in cold water and wiped his face, and he was utterly innocent and utterly good and only sixteen, seventeen at the most, and his hand lay open. But he was absolutely dead, except that he breathed. His head lolled back helplessly when I tried to raise him up. Eventually I picked him up and carried him in my arms to his room, all the way to his bed. His brother was asleep in the other bed and never stirred. I relieved him of his coat and took off his shoes and loosened his clothing here and there, but could not bring myself to undress a sixteen-year-old boy completely, were he ever so dead.

Instead, I went up to my room to sleep.

---

*Icelandic schnapps (*brennivín*), made from concentrated alcohol and water, flavoured with aniseed oil. The nickname comes from the black label on the bottle.

3

THE HOUSE BEHIND THE BUILDINGS

Behind the largest buildings in the town centre there stood a small house which could not be seen from any street, and which no one would imagine existed. A stranger would argue, even swear on oath, that there was no house there. But there was one all the same, a ribbed wooden house, just one little storey and loft, sagging with age – a relic of the old market-town of Reikevig. Angelica and chervil, tansies and dock, ran riot in the garden, so that one could just make out the tumble-down mouldering palings here and there among this tall forest of weeds, still green and juicy although autumn was now well advanced. I never thought I would find this house, but in the end I did.

At first there seemed to be no sign of life about it, but on closer examination a pale streak of light could be seen at a window. I looked for the front door, but the house was set at an angle to the other buildings; at last I found the entrance, round at the back opposite the retaining wall of a large building – the street had probably run that way in days gone by when the house was originally built. I opened the door and entered a dark passageway. At one point a gleam of light showed through a crack between door and jamb, and I knocked. After a brief moment the door was opened, and there stood a slim man of indeterminate age except that every other hair was going grey; and somehow I felt that he knew me the moment he looked at me with those clear expressive eyes, at once mocking and affectionate, from under his bushy eyebrows. I took off my glove and greeted him, and he bade me please enter.

"Was it here?" I asked.

"Yes, here it was," he said, and laughed as if he were making fun of me, or rather of himself perhaps, but quite without malice. I hesitated about walking in and repeated, in the form of a question, the words of the newspaper advertisement:

"Organ-playing for beginners after ten at night?"

"Organ-playing," he said, and kept on looking at me with a smile. "The organ-play of life."

Inside, he had a coal-fire burning in a stove; he did not use the municipal central-heating system. The furniture consisted merely of a host of green plants, some of them in bloom, and a battered three-legged sofa with torn upholstery; and a little harmonium in the corner. A door into another room stood ajar and through it came streaming an aroma of many fragrances; the door to the kitchen was wide open and through it could be seen a table and a few backless chairs and stools, and a kettle on the boil. The air was a little heavy from the flowers, and there was more than a suggestion of smoke seeping from the stove. On one wall hung a coloured print of some creature which might have been a girl had the head not been cleft down to the shoulders; she was bald, her eyes were closed, her profile was superimposed on one half of her face, and she was kissing herself on the mouth. And she had eleven fingers. I stared at the picture dumbfounded.

"Are you a farm girl?" he asked.

"Yes, indeed I am," I replied.

"Why do you want to learn the organ?"

At first I said that I had always listened to music on the wireless, but when I thought it over I felt that this answer was too ordinary, so I corrected myself and added, "I am thinking of playing in our church at home in the north when it is completed."

"May I see your hand?" he said. I consented, and he studied my hand and said, "You have a good hand, but on the large side for music." He himself had a slim, long-fingered hand, very soft to the touch but somehow quite neutral and uncharged with electricity, so that I did not blush even when he fondled the joints of my fingers; nor indeed did I find it disagreeable either.

"Excuse me, but what faith is to be preached in this church at your home in the north?" he asked.

"Oh, I don't suppose it will be anything very remarkable," I said. "Just the same old Lutheran faith, I suppose."

"I don't know what is remarkable if it isn't meeting a girl who is an adherent of Lutheranism," he said. "It has never happened to me before. Do have a seat."

"Luther?" I asked hesitantly as I sat down. "Isn't he ours?"

"I don't know," said the man. "I have only known one man who read Luther; he was a psychologist and was writing a thesis on pornography. Luther, as a matter of fact, is considered the most obscene writer in world literature. A few years ago, when a translation was made of a treatise he wrote about the poor Pope, it was impossible to get it published anywhere on the grounds of indecency. Won't you have a cup of coffee?"

I thanked him but said it was really quite unnecessary, and added that perhaps I would stop playing for this scandalous person Luther if he was such a coarse man, and decide just to play for myself instead. "But that picture over there," I said, for I could not take my eyes off it. "What is it meant to be?"

"Don't you feel it is marvellous?" he said.

"I feel I could do that sort of thing myself – if . . . Excuse me, but is it meant to be a person?"

He replied, "Some say it is Skarpheðinn* after he had been cleft to the shoulders by the axe *Battle-Troll*; others say it is the birth of Cleopatra."

I said it could hardly be Skarpheðinn for he died, as everyone knew, with his axe beside him in the Burning of Njáll. "But who's Cleopatra?" I asked. "It wouldn't be the queen whom Julius Caesar married just before he was murdered?"

"No, it's the other Cleopatra," said the organist, "the one

*Eldest son of Njáll, in the medieval prose epic *Njáll's Saga*.

Napoleon went to visit at Waterloo. When he saw the battle was lost he said "*Merde*" and put on his white gloves and went to visit a woman in a house nearby."

Through the half-open door, from the inner room, came a woman's voice: "He never speaks the truth." And out sailed a large handsome woman, heavily made up and with belladonna in her eyes, wearing sheer stockings, red shoes, and a hat so wide-brimmed that she had to tilt her head to get through the door. She kissed the organist on the ear in farewell as she walked past, and said to me as if in explanation of why he never spoke the truth, "As a matter of fact, he is above God and men. And now I'm off to the Yanks."

The organist brought out a white handkerchief, wiped the moist lipstick from his ear, smiling, and said, "That was she."

At first I thought this was his wife or at least his sweetheart, but when he said "That was she" I was not very clear what he was getting at, for we had been talking about the woman Napoleon went to visit when he saw that the battle was lost.

But while I was pondering this, another woman came through the same door; this one was very old and lame, wearing a soiled flannel nightgown with her grey hair done up in two thin plaits, and she was toothless. She brought out a cheese-rind and a teaspoon on a patterned cake-dish, laid this offering on my knee and called me her dear one, bade me please eat and asked me about the weather. And when she saw that I was in difficulties with the cheese-rind and teaspoon she patted me pityingly on both cheeks with the back of her hand, looked at me with tears in her eyes and said, "Poor blessed creature." These words of compassion she repeated over and over again.

The organist went to her, kissed her, and led her gently and affectionately back into her room; then he relieved me of the cake-dish with its cheese-rind and teaspoon and said, "I am her child."

TWO GODS

He laid a cloth over the kitchen table and put out a few cups and saucers, mostly unmatching; then he brought some twisted, dried-up pastries cut into slices, a few broken biscuits, some sugar but no cream. I knew from the smell of the coffee-pot that he had not been sparing with the coffee. He said that I was to have the only matching cup and saucer. I asked if he were expecting visitors, for he had laid the table for many, but this he flatly denied, except that two gods had promised to make an appearance around midnight. We began to drink the coffee. He urged the meagre baking on me like a hospitable country woman, but laughed at me when I tasted some of it just to please him.

How I was beginning to long to know this man better, converse with him at length, ask him many things about this world and other worlds! – but especially about himself, who he was and why he was the way he was. But my tongue tied itself in knots. It was he who took up the thread again: "As we were saying, I have no time during the day, but you are welcome to come late in the evening or early in the morning."

I said, "Excuse me, but what is your work during the day?"

"I dream," he said.

"All day?" I asked.

"I get up late," he said. "Would you care to hear something on the gramophone?"

He went into the inner room and I heard him winding up a gramophone, and then the needle started running and sound came. At first I thought the instrument was out of order, for nothing could be heard except thuds and thumps, rattle and clatter; but when the organist came back with such an air of sincerity, and exulting as if he himself were the composer, I was sure that everything was as it should be. But nonetheless I started sweating; again and again all sorts of tearing sounds rose above the growling background, and all at once I understood what a dog feels like when it hears a mouth-organ being played and starts to howl. I wanted to yell, and at any rate I would have panted and screwed up my face if the organist had not been sitting on the other side of the table, looking devout and alight with joy.

"Well then?" he asked, when he had stopped the gramophone.

I said, "I don't know what I am to say."

"Did you not feel you could have done that sort of thing yourself?"

"Yes, I can't deny that – if I had had a few tin cans and a couple of pot lids, say. And a cat."

He said, smiling, "It is a characteristic of great art that people who know nothing feel they could have done it themselves – if they were stupid enough."

"Was that beautiful, then?" I asked. "Have I such an ugly soul?"

"Our times, our life – that is our beauty," he said. "Now you have heard the dance of the fire-worshippers."

As these words were being spoken the front door was opened and there came a sound of much traffic in the passageway, until a pram was wheeled into the room by a young man; and this was god number one.

This incarnate spirit was tall and well-built and handsome in his way, wearing a herring-bone overcoat and with his tie carefully knotted in the way which only town people know and country people can never learn; he was bare-headed, with wavy hair parted in the middle, gleaming and smelling strongly of brilliantine. He nodded to me and looked directly at me; his eyes glowed piercingly, and he gave me the savage smile which people smile at those they are going to murder – later; and bared those splendid teeth. He steered the pram into the middle of the room and then propped up among the flowers a long flat triangular object wrapped in paper and tied up with packthread. Then he came over and offered me a clammy hand and mumbled something which sounded to me like "Jesus Christ"; I thought he smelled of fish. Perhaps he said "Jens

Kristinsson"; anyway I returned his greeting and stood up according to the custom of country women. Then I peeped into the pram, and there slept a pair of real twins.

"This is the god Brilliantine," said the organist.

"My goodness, to have these darling little children out so late at night!" I said. "Where's their mother?"

"She's south in Keflavík," said the god. "There's a Yank dance."

"Children survive everything," said the organist. "Some think it harmful for children to lose their mother, but that is a fallacy. Even though they lose their father it has no ill effect on them. Here's some coffee. Where's the atom poet, if I may ask?"

"He's in the Cadillac," said the god.

"And where is Two Hundred Thousand Pliers?" asked the organist.

"F.F.F.," said the god. "New York, 34th Street, 1250."

"No new metaphysical discoveries, no great mystic visions, no religious revelations?" asked the organist.

"Bugger-all," said the god. "Except this character Óli Figure. He says he's made contact with the Nation's Darling.* The snot's dribbling from his nose. Who's this girl?"

"You as a god should not ask about people," said the organist. "It is ungodly. It is a secret who a person is. And even more of a secret what a person is called. The old god never asked who a person was and what he or she was called."

"Is Cleopatra better of the clap yet?" asked the god.

"Better, in what way?" asked the organist.

"I visited her in hospital," said the god. "She was bad."

"I do not know what you mean," said the organist.

"Ill," said the god.

"A person is never too ill," said the organist.

"She was screaming," said the god.

"Suffering and happiness are two matters so alike that it

*Jónas Hallgrímsson (1807–1845), Iceland's greatest Romantic poet, who inspired the nineteenth-century nationalist revival.

is impossible to distinguish between them," said the organist. "The greatest enjoyment I know is to be ill, especially very ill."

Then a voice was heard from the doorway, saying in fanatically religious tones, "How I wish I could at last get that cancer now."

The newcomer was so young that his face was the colour of ivory, with only a trace of down on his cheeks: a youthful portrait of a foreign genius, a postcard like the ones which hang above the harmonium in the country and which can be bought in the village of Sanðárkrókur – a mixture of Schiller, Schubert and Lord Byron, with a bright red tie and dirty shoes. He looked around with the sudden strained expression of the sleepwalker, and every object, whether animate or inanimate, affected him like an overwhelming mystical vision. He offered me his long thin hand, which was so limp that I felt I could crush it into pulp, and said, "I am Benjamin."

I looked at him.

"Yes, I know it," he said. "But I can't help it. This little brother, it is I; this terrible tribe, it is my people; this desert – my country."

"They have read the Holy Scriptures," said the organist, "and the Holy Spirit has enlightened them in their reading, in accordance with the precepts of our friend Luther: they have found the godhead without the mediation of the Pope. Have a cup of coffee, atom poet."

"Where's Cleopatra?" asked Benjamin the atom poet.

"Never mind that," said the organist. "Help yourselves to sugar with your coffee."

"I admire her," said the atom poet.

"And I need to see her too," said the god Brilliantine.

"Why should she be wanting to run around with two gods?" said the organist. "She wants to have her thirty men."

I could no longer contain myself and blurted out, "Now really! – I am no model of virtue, but never have I heard tell of so immoral a woman, and I permit myself to doubt whether such a woman exists."

"Immoral women do not exist," said the organist. "That is only a superstition. On the other hand there exist women who sleep thirty times with one man, and women who sleep once with thirty men."

"And women who don't sleep with a man at all," I said, meaning myself in fact, and had begun to sweat; and there was a mist before my eyes and I was undoubtedly blushing all the way down to my neck and making myself utterly absurd.

"Augustine, one of the Fathers of the Church, says that the sexual urge is beyond the will," said the organist. "Saint Benedict gratified it by throwing himself naked into a bed of nettles. There are no sexual perversions other than celibacy."

"May I see you home?" said the god Brilliantine.

"What for?" I asked.

"There are Yanks around at night," he said.

"What does that matter?" I said.

"They have guns."

"I'm not scared of guns."

"They will rape you," he said.

"Are you going to fight for me?"

"Yes," he said, and smiled his piercing smile.

"What about the children?"

"Benjamin can take them in the Cadillac," he said. "Or if you like I shall beat Benjamin up and take the Cadillac off him. I have just as much right to steal the Cadillac as he has."

"I'm going to look for Cleopatra," said Benjamin the atom poet.

"One tune first," said the organist. "There's no hurry."

The god Brilliantine rose to his feet and brought out the flat triangular object which he had propped up amongst the flowers, loosened the twine and unwrapped the paper. It was a salted fish. He tied the twine most artistically to make two strings running the length of the fish, and started strumming on them. With his right hand he made agile flourishes as if he were striking the strings, and one could hear a sound like a guitar being played, a Hawaiian guitar. He was crooning limply through his mouth and nose, and the guitar sound was made by plucking his nose between his thumb and forefinger in mid-flourish and checking the air in his nostrils. The atom poet stepped to the middle of the floor and began to strike an attitude. He had all the gestures of the world's greatest. It had not occurred to me that he could sing, and I was all the more surprised when he opened his mouth: a singer, with the bright and the sombre blended in his voice; an actor, more-over, who knew the anguish of the soul and could imitate the sobbing of the Italians. He turned to face me:

> You are a dream but a little too plump,
> You are virtuous but just for a time,
> You are an innocent country lump
> Closely akin to the awfullest crime;
> And I hate you just about none,
> The same at the last as the first,
> I break out to you, in I burst,
> Through atom and moon, earth and the sun.

While the accompaniment was ending he put his hand casu-ally into his pocket; and it seemed as if he had been carrying eggs in it and they had broken and his hand had become all covered with muck – was this play-acting? The only certain thing was that he began to pull out of his pockets vast sums of money, bunch after bunch of bank-notes, 10 krónur notes, 50 and 100 krónur notes;* and in a sudden fit he began to tear the notes in two, crumpling up the pieces and throwing them on the floor and grinding them down like a man killing an insect. Then he sat down and lit a cigarette.

The god Brilliantine continued to play until the postlude was finished. The organist first laughed, rather affectionately, then fetched a brush and dustpan and swept the floor, emptied

---

*Icelandic currency is based on the *króna* (pl. *krónur*); the *króna* has 100 *aurar* (sing. *eyrir*).

the dustpan into the fire, thanked them for the song, and offered more coffee. The twins had woken up and started to cry.

THEOLOGICAL NIGHT-WALK

The atom poet drove away in the Cadillac, that aristocratic car the like of which I had never seen. The god Brilliantine was left behind with the crying twins, and myself.

"Now I shall see you home," he said.

"Would it not be more to the point for me to help you with the twins?" I said.

"Leave them to themselves," he said.

"Whose are these twins, if I may ask?" I said. "Aren't they yours?"

"They are my wife's," he said.

"Well, anyway," I said, "there's no sense in letting them cry."

I tried as far as I could to console the poor things out there in the street in the drizzle in the middle of the night. A crowd of drunks gathered round us. After a little while the mites went to sleep. I wanted to go off on my own then, but it turned out that the god and I were going the same way westwards.

When we had walked for a while along the road I could not restrain myself from asking, "Was that real money, or was it fake?"

"There is no such thing as real money," he said. "All money is fake. We gods spit on money."

"But the atom poet must surely be well off to be driving such a car."

"All those who know how to steal are well off," said the god. "All those who don't know how to steal are badly off. The problem is to know how to steal."

I wanted to know where and how that little poet had stolen that huge car.

"From whom but our master, Pliers?" said the god. "What,

you haven't heard of Pliers? Two Hundred Thousand Pliers? F.F.F.? The man who sits in New York and fakes the figures for the joint-stock company, Snorredda, and the rest? And wrote an article in the papers about the next world and built a church in the north?"

"You must forgive me if I'm a little slow on the uptake," I said. "I'm from the country."

"There's no difficulty in understanding it," he said. "F.F.F.: in English, the Federation of Fulminating Fish, New York; in Icelandic, the Figures-Faking-Federation. One button costs half an eyrir over there in the west, but you have a company in New York, the F.F.F., which sells you the button at 2 krónur and writes on the invoice: button, 2 krónur. You make a profit of 4000%. After a month you're a millionaire. You can understand that?"

Suddenly we heard someone hailing us, and a man came running up behind us, bare-headed. It was the organist.

"Sorry," he said, out of breath with running. "I forgot something. I don't suppose one of you could possibly lend me a króna?"

The god found nothing in his pockets, but I had a króna in my coat pocket and let the organist have it. He thanked me and apologised and said that he would repay me the next time: "You see, I need to buy myself 50 grams of boiled sweets tomorrow morning," he said. Then he bade us goodnight and left.

We walked on in silence for a while with the pram, and now it was past midnight. I was busy with my thoughts, trying to fathom the night's events, until my companion said, "Don't you think I'm rather different from other men, actually?"

He was certainly very handsome and must undoubtedly have charmed many girls with those piercing eyes and that moist murderer's smile, but somehow he had no effect on me at all; I scarcely even heard him when he was saying something.

"Fortunately no two men are alike," I said.

"Yes, but don't you feel an uncanny current coming from me?" he asked.

"If you yourself feel that an uncanny current comes from you, isn't that enough?" I said.

"I have always felt that I was different from others," he said. "I felt it when I was small. I felt that there was a soul in me. I saw the world from a height of many thousand metres. Even when I was thrashed it was of no concern to me; I could tuck Reykjavík under my arm and go away with it."

"It must be strange to have such notions," I said. "I find it difficult to understand, for I have never had strange notions myself."

"It comes naturally to me," he said. "Anything which others say is of no concern to me. I am above them all; above everything. I can't help looking upon others with a smile."

"Just so," I said.

He went on, "I feel that the godhead and I are one. I feel that I and Jesus and Muhammad and Bu . . . Buddhy are one."

"Can you prove it?" I asked.

"I was born with it," he said. "At first, for a long time, I thought that others had it too and that everyone was mad. I started to ask the other boys. But they didn't understand me. Then it turned out that no one had it except me; and Benjamin; we two had it."

"Had what?" I asked.

"A soul," he said. "A divine, eternal soul; that means that God and I are one. You go out to steal, perhaps you kill someone; it doesn't concern you, you are a soul, you are part of God. You are beaten up, but that doesn't concern you either, especially if you are badly beaten up; or you land in a life or death fight; or the police cosh you on the head and then hand-cuff you – despite that, you are utterly happy and have nobody. In the morning you appear in court, but your soul rests in God; you are thrown into jail, but you are aware of nothing, you understand nothing except Jesus and Muhammad and . . . what was the name of the third one again? You hear only this one voice which always whispers: 'You are I and I am you.' I am also utterly happy even though I am not beaten up, heaven and earth are open before me, nothing can hurt me, I understand everything and can do everything, own everything and may do everything."

"I feel," I said, "that if you are what you say you are, you must show some token of it." But he did not understand what I meant by a token, so I added in explanation: "Perform a miracle."

He said: "No man on earth can play a salted fish except me. If I wanted to I could go to Hollywood and become a millionaire."

I did not say a word, and he took my arm and pulled me towards him and looked at me: "Aren't you at all amazed? Haven't you fallen for me at all? Listen, come on behind the buildings with me, I want to tell you something."

I don't know what sort of a fool I was, to go wandering with him behind a house; for of course before I knew it he had put me up against a wall and had started kissing me and trying to pull my skirt up, with the pram standing nearby. I was slow in getting my hands up to hit him, but as I gathered my wits I said, "No you don't, my lad, even if you're a treble god and your head plastered with brilliantine too." Then I struck him, kicked him and pushed him away.

"You damned bitch," he said. "Don't you know I can murder you?"

"Didn't I know you were a murderer?" I said. "I knew it the moment I set eyes on you."

"Then you can stare into the barrel of this," he said, suddenly flourishing something in front of my face; I could not see what it was in the dark, but it could well have been a revolver for all I knew.

Someone in the house opened a window above us and asked what the devil we were up to, this was his ground, and told us to hop it or else he would call the police. The god Brilliantine thrust the revolver back into his pocket, if revolver it was, and wheeled the pram back to the road.

"I was just testing you," he said. "You can more or less imagine whether I meant anything, a penniless father of a family like me. Now I'll see you home."

But then he suddenly remembered something: "Have I not gone and forgotten that damned salted fish? The wife's sure to beat me if I don't bring her some food for tomorrow."

He ran back through the gate to fetch this sustenance for his family, and I made off while he was looking for the fish.

4

PERSUASIONS

When my mother became sixty she was given 100 krónur. It then turned out that she could not recognise money. She had never seen money before. On the other hand, the day had never dawned since she was twelve years old that she had worked less than sixteen hours out of twenty-four during the winter, and eighteen during the summer, unless she were ill. So it was little wonder that I felt I must have been drunk the previous evening, or in a cinema, to see all that money torn up and then burned.

Madam awoke for her hot chocolate at 11 a.m. and sat up in the huge big bed, glowing with happiness that there should be no justice in the world, and began to drink that sweet fatty brew and read the Conservative paper; for it was little wonder that the woman should think this a splendid world and want to conserve it. When I was on my way out again she cleared her throat delicately and told me to wait. She did nothing in haste, she drank up slowly and finished the article she was reading. When she had drunk and read her fill she got out of bed, slipped a dressing-gown on and sat down in front of the mirror with the back of her head towards me, and started to do herself up.

"You are a young girl from the country," she said.

I did not say much to that.

"Naturally it doesn't concern me at all how my maids spend their nights," she said. "But for the sake of the house – you understand?"

"For the sake of the house?" I said.

"Exactly, for the sake of the house," she said. "A maid once brought lice into the house."

Then she turned round on the seat and looked me all over and smiled and said, "Cavaliers are not all the same."

"Indeed?" I said.

"Very much so," she said, still giving me that searching look, with a smile on her lips.

"So now I know," I said.

"So now you know," she said, and began to study her own reflection again. "My husband and I said nothing last year even though the maid brought in a Yank now and again; they get health inspections. We preferred that to having her sleeping out somewhere, for instance with some louse-ridden seaman."

Why did she say "my husband and I"? Had they lain awake for the housemaid, clock in hand? Or was she reminding me of the difference between lying married in a moral bed at home and being an outcast? She had long scarlet-painted nails, and I felt sure she scratched her husband. Originally I had intended to tell her the whole story about my night out the previous evening, but now all at once I felt that I had no call to explain myself to this woman.

"But we shall hang on to the hope," she said, "that you haven't landed up in one of those cells."

"Cells?" – I said I did not understand the word.

"All the more dangerous for you," she said. "Country girls who do not read the papers, and don't understand what's going on in the community, land up in a cell before they know of it."

"Really, I'm becoming almost curious," I said.

"No words can describe the bestiality of Communists," she said.

"I'll soon be almost taking a fancy to bestiality if you go on talking like this," I said.

"No other girl in the whole country was in greater danger than I," she said solemnly. "My father owns wholesale businesses and retail businesses, cinemas, trawlers, printing works, newspapers, fish oil factories and bone meal factories; I could do anything and I was allowed to do anything; I could have gone to Paris any time I liked and taken part in whatever bestiality I fancied; I could even have become a Communist if I had wanted to, and fought to tear the shirt from my father's back. But yet I did not land up in any bestiality. I met my man and with him have built my house. I have given birth to my children, my girl, and it has been my life's work to bring them up for the community. No honourable woman regrets having given birth to her children and brought them up, instead of abandoning herself to bestiality."

VISITORS BY NIGHT

That evening she told me to look my best, for there were some distinguished men from America coming to talk to her husband. She said that I was to open the door for them and invite them in, but warned me not to greet them or look at them and above all not to look welcoming, because foreigners misunderstood such things. If I knew no English it was safest just to be silent; and I should be particularly careful not to say "Please" when I brought them soda-water. "My husband will see to the whisky," she said.

I waited half-anxiously throughout the evening for these guests who were so high class that they could be soiled if an ordinary person greeted them. At last they arrived. Their car sped up to the front gate and was speeding away again almost at once, and they on the doorstep with a finger on the bell; I opened the door and let them in. One was a stout man in general's uniform, the other a lanky man in civilian clothes. I had expected them not to look at me, much less sully themselves by offering a greeting, but it was not like that at all: these men were kindliness itself and it was as if they had met an old girlfriend. They smiled genially and talked nineteen to the dozen; one of them patted me on the back; there was no question of my having to hang up their coats and headgear for them, they did that for themselves. The general, moreover, dug into his pocket for a handful of chewing gum and gave it to me, and the other, not to be outdone, gave me a packet of cigarettes. To tell the truth, I had hardly ever met more affable people, and yet so free and easy; so much so that I forgot all the stiff manners which had been impressed upon me, and I smiled and was their friend. When I brought them the soda-water and glasses a moment later they were seated beside the master of the house with maps in front of them, both of Iceland and the world. The master stood up and came towards me and helped me to put down the tray and asked me to be at hand in case they should need anything with it, but they required nothing all evening. Near midnight their car came up to the gate and they rushed off; for some reason it was not considered a good idea to let their car pause for any length of time outside the house.

Very few minutes passed before there was another visitor on the porch. This was the first time I had seen the Prime Minister, Madam's brother; I knew only that he lived in the corner house a minute away down the street, but I recognised him from his pictures. He did not give me so much as a glance when I opened the door, but more or less barged through me into the house, still wearing his hat. When I took in a glass and cold soda-water for him, the master said in his very Icelandic way, "And this is our mountain-owl from the north." But the Prime Minister lit himself a cigar, his shoulders hunched, with an expression on his face of pained constipation, full of assumed profundity, and made no reply to such trivialities.

From midnight onwards more and more visitors filtered in; I suspected that the Prime Minister had been telephoning and rousing them from sleep. Some of them were the kind of people who give the impression that the centre of the universe is always where they themselves happen to be. They sat in the Doctor's study and talked in low tones, and did not get drunk. I was told that I should go to bed, but far into the night I felt that the house was some sort of clandestine marketplace.

ICELAND IN THE STREET. THE YOUTH CENTRE

At dusk the next day I went to the baker's shop on the corner opposite the Prime Minister's house; there was always a pensive girl standing there behind the counter serving milk and bread, and sometimes there was a young man standing in front of it, talking to her. And suddenly there was unrest in this restful street, with loosely-knit groups of young people milling around in front of the Prime Minister's house; something had happened, there was vehemence in their eyes, and no one was smiling. Curious passers-by paused on the pavement, and windows in the vicinity were thrown open. Under a lamp-post stood two policemen with black helmets and truncheons; and I don't suppose it was burnt cork they had smeared around their eyes?

"What's this?" I said to a dignified-looking man who was hurrying along the street with a profound air. He replied tersely, "It's the Communists," and vanished. Now I began to get curious in earnest, and put the same question to someone in grubby overalls; he looked at me in amazement at first, then replied rather brusquely as he turned away, "The country is to be sold."

"Who's going to sell the country?" I said aloud to myself out in the middle of the street, and people looked at me in surprise. After a little while I heard the groups of young people start to shout at the Prime Minister's house, "We don't want to sell Iceland, we don't want to sell Iceland."

Some young man climbed on to the wall in front of the house and began to harangue the Prime Minister's windows, but the police walked over to him and told him to stop, since there was no one at home – the family had gone to the country for the day. Little by little the youth stopped making his speech, but someone suggested we should sing "Our Fjord-riven Fatherland", and this was done. Soon the youth contingents drifted away, heading down town, still singing; the people on the pavements dispersed, and the windows in the vicinity were closed again.

The baker's shop was still open, the girl still behind the counter and the young man in front of it; they were looking very serious, with large clear eyes, and did not notice when I said Good evening.

"Was that the Communists?" I asked.

"Huh?" said the girl, coming to with a start and glancing at the boy.

"It was the Teachers' Training College and the Young Men's Christian Association," the boy said.

"What's happened?" I asked.

He asked whether I did not read the newspapers, but I laughed and said that I was from the north. Then he showed me an article in the evening paper which said that a request had been received from one of the Great Powers that Iceland should sell, lend, or give it her capital city, Reykjavík, otherwise named Smoky Bay, or some other bay equally suitable for attack or defence in an atomic war. I was speechless at such nonsense and asked in my innocence if this were not the same as everything else one read in newspapers: one of the first things I had been taught as a child was never to believe a single word written in newspapers.

"Listen," he said, "don't you want to take part in a lottery in aid of the Youth Centre? You can go round the world in an aeroplane."

"Or get a sewing machine," added the girl.

"I have no wish to go round the world," I said. "And I can't do anything with my hands."

"But you want a Youth Centre?" said the boy.

"What for?" I asked.

"You're from the north, I'm from the west, and there's no Youth Centre," said the boy.

"So what?" I asked.

"Every cultural subject in the world is pursued in a Youth Centre," he said. "The Icelandic nation should be the best educated and the noblest nation in the world. Capitalism says that Iceland's youth should be like the wild horses which are never given shelter. That is wrong. Iceland's youth should have the largest Centre in the country."

"What does it cost?" I asked.

"Millions," he said.

"I have 25 krónur," I said. I had been thinking of buying myself some underclothes.

"Aren't you with Búi Árland's wife?" asked the girl. I said yes.

"Don't say another word," said the boy. "The ones who have the Thieves' Company in New York? They could build a Youth Centre on their own with the money they have stolen from us with their fraudulent price-scales all through the war. Take about ten tickets."

"Would it not be better for me to support the church my father is going to build up north in Eystridalur?" I asked.

Up to this point they had both been earnest, but now all at once they were amused; they looked at one another and burst out laughing.

STORM IN A SOUP PLATE

During dinner I asked if anyone wanted to buy raffle tickets in aid of a Youth Centre. Such a jest had never been heard at that table since the new maid announced that she was going to learn to play the harmonium. Soup spouted from the mouths of the two middle children. The eldest son, who was a full-time employee of Universal Suffering, Inc., contented himself with throwing me a look of mingled pity and nausea. Madam looked at me speechlessly at first, and then cleared her throat ominously; her husband woke up from his newspaper, looking tired as if he had not slept well, and said, "Huh?"

"She's selling tickets for a Youth Centre," said the little fat boy.

The Doctor asked to see them and I showed him a ticket – on one side a picture of a Centre and on the other a picture of the prizes offered.

"Thank you," he said, and returned the ticket to me with that tired smile of his; but I was glad to see a gleam in his spectacles and a glimpse of his white teeth. "We had this in Parliament," he said. "And we also had it in the Town Council."

"Where did you get these chits, my dear, if I may ask?" said Madam.

"I was out at the baker's during the disturbance and met the girl there . . ."

Madam interrupted me and said, "I've heard she's a Communist."

". . . There was a young man with her who asked if I would take a few tickets," I said.

"They're Communists," said Madam.

"What happened out there during the disturbance, by the way?" asked her husband.

"Oh, there wasn't much of a disturbance really," I said.

"Yes, there was," said Fatty. "It was the Communists."

"There was a small crowd of people who were saying, 'We don't want to sell the country'. I was told that it was the Teachers' Training College and the Christian Association."

Madam said, "Oh, is that so, indeed? That settles it, then! Always when they spread the word that it was someone else you can be sure that it was them. They know how to egg fools on. Teachers' Training College and the Christian Association, indeed! Why not the Woman's Emancipation Society and the China Mission? I advise you to rid yourself of these tickets as quickly as you can. This Youth Centre – it's a cell building."

"Let me see them," said little Fatty. "Let me have them."

I was standing behind the chair of the elder daughter of the house; and before I knew it she dug her nails fiercely into my legs just behind the knee and darted her icy-hot look at me, without giving me the least idea whether she was in favour of a Youth Centre or not.

In all innocence, I handed the boy a ticket.

"All of them," he said.

But just as he was reaching out for them a hand glittering with diamonds and bracelets came swooping through the air and snatched them from me. It was Madam. In a twinkling she had torn them to pieces, across and down, and tossed the shreds behind her through the open folding doors into the next room. With this done she looked at me coldly and said without endearments, "If you start any Communist propaganda in this house again I shall dismiss you."

Then she took a spoonful of soup.

It was the elder son's habit to smoke between courses. He brought out a cigarette; he was frowning heavily, his mouth pulled down at the corners in infinite disgust after the soup.

"There's no point in getting excited, Mother," he said. "Fascism has been tried, and it didn't work. Communism will conquer the world. Everyone knows that. *Rien à faire.*"

She straightened in her chair, looked directly at him, and said to him with icy porcelain severity, "My boy, the time has come to send you to an asylum."

"Did I create this world you brought me into?" asked the boy dispassionately, and went on smoking.

"And it's high time I told you a few more things, my child," she began, working herself up to eagle heights, so that her husband woke up again from his newspaper, smiled, and laid his palm on the back of her hand. This interrupted her flow and she turned on him instead. "You smile!" she said. "Yes, you probably have a very nice smile, but unfortunately it's a little out of place here."

"My dearest Dúlla," said her husband, imploringly.

I left the dining room and did not stop when I reached the kitchen; I walked straight up to my room in the middle of the family's soup course and started thinking. Was it not best for me to pack up and go? But when I began to gather up my few possessions I remembered that I had nowhere definite to stay the night if I left; and no place for the harmonium. How much can one sacrifice for the sake of one's pride? Everything, of course – if one is proud enough. There is nothing as wretched as letting oneself be trampled upon, except spending the night out of doors. Then the cook was standing in the doorway, saying, In the name of Jesus, was I not going to hurry in with the gratin?

When I came back to the dining room, having recovered from my anger, the family had finished with the soup and were being strenuously silent. The Doctor was reading his paper again. I cleared the dishes and brought in the next course and went out. The raffle tickets for the Youth Centre lay on the floor, and I left them there.

In the evening the house was silent. The middle children went out to stand at the corner of the house with the Prime Minister's children and other better-class offspring to jeer at the passers-by; it was a game they could enjoy for hours at a time in the evenings. The elder son vanished to some unknown destination. The cook's God-fearing elf-child had two mechanical dolls which could wet their nappies, known as piddle dolls, which the little darling had to tend carefully before she began on her Jesus chants. Madam had gone out to a party to play the kind of whist they call bridge, in which the players tell each other what they have in their hands before the first card is laid. And I had long since calmed down.

When I had been sitting for a good while at the harmonium, struggling with these big disobedient fingers of mine which are so ignorant of any art, I finally came to and noticed that my door was open and that there was a man standing in the doorway. I thought at first I was having hallucinations. He was looking at me with his eyes puckered up a little, and was polishing his spectacles; and smiling. First I went cold, then I went hot. I stood up but there was no strength in my knees; a mist swam before my eyes. And I swear a sacred oath this had never happened to me before.

"I heard music," he said.

"You shouldn't make fun of . . ."

He asked who my teacher was, and I mentioned the organist's ordinary sounding name.

"Has he become an organist too now?" said Doctor Búi Árland. "Yes, well, why not? He was always far ahead of the rest of us; so far ahead that he got into the habit of sleeping all day so as not to have to look upon this stupid criminal society."

"He grows flowers," I said.

"That's nice," said the Doctor. "I wish I grew flowers. While I was reading newspapers, he was reading the Italian Renaissance authors in the original. I can remember him saying that he was going to save the war news for himself until, after twenty years, it would be possible to read about the whole war in two minutes in an encyclopedia. I am glad he grows flowers. Do you think I should send my children to him? Do you think he could make something out of them?"

"You're asking a big question," I said. "You don't seem to realise that I am the most stupid thing there is in the whole of Iceland, and that I don't have opinions about anything – least of all in your hearing."

"You are fully earthed," he said, and smiled. "May I see your hand?" And when he had studied it he said, "A large, well-shaped hand."

And I felt as if I were being roasted, drenched in sweat all over, that he should study my hand.

He slipped his spectacles back on to his nose with a prac-tised gesture. Then he reached into his pocket and brought out a 100 krónur note and gave it to me. "Your raffle tickets," he said.

"They only cost 50 krónur," I said, "and I haven't any change."

"You can get change later," he said.

"I don't accept money for nothing," I said.

"Don't be afraid, everyone pays as little as he can get away with," he said. "It is a natural law; I am a political economist."

"Yes, but then I shall have to get you another ten raffle tickets," I said.

"But preferably don't give me them over the soup," he said, and smiled, and left, and closed the door behind him.

5

AT MY ORGANIST'S

Judging by pictures on postcards, one would think that great musicians had been gods, not men. But now I learned that the world's greatest composers have been the most wretched outcasts of humanity. Schubert was considered by respectable people in Vienna nothing but an uneducated boy who did not even know anything about music; and he revenged himself, indeed, by composing a cheap tune like *Ave Maria* which even country people in the north know; and died of malnutrition at about the age of thirty. Beethoven did not even get a rudimentary petit-bourgeois education; he could only just use a pen, no better than a farmhand; and he wrote a ludicrous letter which is called his Testament. He fell in love with a few countesses, rather like an old hack falling for stud-mares. In the eyes of respectable people in Vienna he was first and foremost just a deaf eccentric, badly dressed and dirty, not fit for decent company. But these two outcasts stood high in society compared with some others of the world's greatest composers.

Many of them were employed by comic-opera kings and were kept to play for them while they were feeding – including Johann Sebastian Bach who, however, wasted even more years quarrelling with the bourgeois riff-raff of Leipzig. Haydn, the world's greatest composer of his time, was frequently beaten by the Esterhazy family, for whom he was an employee for thirty years; he was not even allowed to eat at their table. Mozart, the man who most nearly reached the celestial heights, stood lower in the hierarchy of society than the lap-dogs of the petty kings and oafish bishops who used him as a drudge. When he died of misery and wretchedness in the prime of life, not a living creature followed his coffin to the grave except for one mongrel; people made the excuse that it had been raining; some said they had had influenza.

By now I was asking for the dance of the fire-worshippers: wild men beating drums at night around a pyre out in the rain . . . and suddenly some instrument breaking into a four-note melody with a searing quality which went right through me; and a few days later, in the middle of my work, I would wake to a sudden sweet stab of longing for that wild, brief, blazing melody.

And one day I noticed that there was some hair after all on the head of the cloven girl I had thought bald – light-blue hair, or green rather, thick and greasy. I had not previously noticed that the head and the hair were painted on their own; well, thank goodness all her hair was there for certain – only separated from the head by a white line.

Queen Cleopatra, barefoot, wearing silk panties and a fur coat, with a cigarette in her mouth and covered with make-up, went gliding into the kitchen from the room of the bed-ridden mother of the house.

"I'm beginning to want that coffee," she said.

The organist: "Cleopatra, you own the whole of Brazil, and Turkey, and Java" – and I cannot remember what other coffee-lands he listed.

"Yes, but she hasn't got eleven fingers," I said, and looked at the picture on the wall.

"Who knows," said the organist, "perhaps the eleventh finger is the very finger she lacks even though she deserves to have it?"

"A picture is still a picture," I said.

"And nothing else," he said. "The other day I saw a photograph of a typist, and she has thirty-five fingers."

"Shall I go into the kitchen and count Cleopatra's fingers?" I said.

He said, "A picture is not a girl, even though it is the picture of a girl. One can even say that the more closely a picture resembles a girl, the further it is from being a girl. Everyone wants to sleep with a girl, but no one wants to sleep with the image of a girl. Even an exact wax model of Cleopatra has no bloodstream, and no vagina. You do not like the eleventh finger, but now I shall tell you something: the eleventh finger takes the place of these two things."

When he had said this he looked at me and laughed. Then he leaned over to me and whispered, "Now I am going to let you into the most remarkable secret of all: the image of Cleopatra which resembles her more closely than all other images, namely the person who has just walked through this room and into the kitchen to make some coffee – she of course has a bloodstream and many other nice things, but even so, she is furthest of all from being Cleopatra. Nothing tells one less about Cleopatra than this apparently haphazard but yet logical biochemical synthesis. Even the man who celebrates a silver wedding anniversary with her after twenty-five years of marriage will not know more about her than the one who lay with her for half an hour, or than you who see her for a few seconds crossing a room; the fact is, she is not even a likeness of herself. And this is what the artist knows; and that is why he paints her with eleven fingers."

THE PICTURES IN MY HOUSEHOLD

Next day I stood in the middle of the room beside two domestic animals – an electric floor polisher and a vacuum cleaner –

and began to study the pictures in the house. I had often looked at these 10- or even 20-centimetre mountains which seemed to have been made sometimes of porridge, sometimes of bluish sago pudding, sometimes a mash of curds – sometimes even like an upturned bowl with the glacier Eiríksjökull underneath; and I had never been able to understand where I was meant to be, because anyone who comes from the north and has lived opposite a mountain cannot understand a mountain in a picture in the south.

In this house there hung, so to speak, mountains and mountains and yet more mountains, mountains with glacial caps, mountains by the sea, ravines in mountains, lava below mountains, birds in front of mountains; and still more mountains; until finally these wastelands had the effect of a total flight from habitation, almost a denial of human life. I would not dream of trying to argue that this was not art, especially since I do not have the faintest idea what art is; but if this was art, it was first and foremost the art of those who had sinned against humanity and fled into the wilderness, the art of outlaws. Quite apart from how debased Nature becomes in a picture, nothing seems to me to express so much contempt for Nature as a painting of Nature. I touched the waterfall and did not get wet, and there was no sound of a cascade; over there was a little white cloud, standing still instead of breaking up; and if I sniffed that mountain slope I bumped my nose against a congealed mass and found only a smell of chemicals, at best a whiff of linseed oil; and where were the birds? And the flies? And the sun, so that one's eyes were dazzled? Or the mist, so that one only saw a faint glimmer of the nearest willow shrub? Yes, certainly this was meant to be a farmhouse, but where, pray, was the smell of the cow dung? What is the point of making a picture which is meant to be like Nature, when everyone knows that this is the one thing which a picture cannot be and should not be and must not be? Who thought up the theory that Nature is a matter of sight alone? Those who know Nature hear it rather than see it, feel it rather than hear it; smell it, good heavens, yes – but first and foremost eat it. Certainly Nature is in front of us, and behind us; Nature is under and over us, yes, and in us; but most particularly it exists in time, always changing and always passing, never the same; and never in a rectangular frame.

A farmhouse with a turf roof is not what it looks like from a distance some sunshine night in July; nothing is further from being a farmhouse. I had spent all my childhood in a farm opposite a mountain; it would be no use for anyone who wanted to paint my farm to start from the turf roof, the artist would have to start from the inside and not the outside, start from the minds of those who lived there. And a bird, I also know what a bird is. Oh, those dear divine birds! It may well be that this picture of a bird cost many thousands of krónur but, may I ask, could any honourable person, or any person who appreciates birds at all, justify to his own conscience painting a bird sitting on a stone for all eternity, motionless as a convicted criminal or a country person posing for the photographer at Sanðárkrókur? A bird is first and foremost movement; the sky is part of a bird or, rather, the air and the bird are one; a long journey in a straight line into space, that is a bird; and heat, for a bird is warmer than a human being and has a quicker heartbeat, and is happier besides, as one can hear from its call – for there is no sound like the chirp of a bird and it is not a bird at all if it does not chirp. This soundless bird on a stone, this picture of no movement, no long journey in a straight line, might have been meant to represent the dead stuffed bird which stood on top of a cabinet in our pastor's house at home; or the tin birds one could buy at Sanðárkrókur when I was small. But a picture of a dead bird is not that of a bird, but of death; stuffed death; tin death.

6

THE MINK FARM

One of the most enterprising mink farms in the vicinity had suffered a great loss: fifty minks had been stolen. When I arrived for my organ lesson in the evening, two close friends of the organist's were sitting there, both of them policemen, the one selfconscious and other unselfconscious, both organ pupils. They had come straight from duty and were drinking coffee in the kitchen and arguing over this business.

"What does it matter if fifty minks are stolen?" said the organist.

"What does it matter!" said the unselfconscious policeman. "The rascals didn't even have the sense to cut off their heads, the beasts are roaming around at large. A mink is a mink. It kills chickens. And destroys trout and birds. And attacks lambs. Do you want to have everything in the country stolen? Do you want to have your chamber pot stolen from you?"

"People should have solid and immovable privies," said the organist, "not unsecured chamber pots."

"Yes, but what if you had a gold chamber pot? Or at any rate a silver chamber pot?" said the unselfconscious policeman.

"Some penniless innocent manages, after strenuous efforts, to break into a small shop and steal some shoelaces and malt extract," said the organist. "Or manages to remove an old coat from a vestibule, or sneak into a dairy through the back door and grab the loose change left over in the till the night before, or pinch the wallet off a drunken seaman, or dip into a farm-hand's travel box and take his summer pay. It is perhaps possible to steal our tin chamber pots, although only by special dispensation of God's grace. But it is impossible to steal our gold chamber pots, or even our silver ones; for they are properly guarded. No, life would be fun if one could just walk out and steal a million whenever one was broke."

"There's no need to go as far as saying they empty all the banks and the Treasury," said the unselfconscious policeman.

"I have two friends who never spurned a carelessly locked door or a back window off the snib at night," said the organist. "By constant night vigils for two years, and all the diligence and conscientiousness it is possible to apply to one's work, they managed to scrape together a sum equivalent to half a year's pay for a dustman. Then they spent another two years in jail; eight man-years' work, all told. If such people are dangerous, then at least they are a danger to no one but themselves. I am rather afraid that my friend Búi Árland and the others in F.F.F. would think that a poor return over eight years."

"Yet his son goes out and steals fifty minks," said the unselfconscious policeman.

"My God!" I said. "Búi Árland's son!"

They noticed me then for the first time, and the organist came over to me and greeted me, and the two men introduced themselves; one of them was a cheery, broad-beamed man, the other a serious young man with hot eyes which peered at you stealthily. The police had got wind that little Þórður Árland, the one called Bóbó, and a friend of his, had stolen these fifty beasts; they had slaughtered some of them down by the Elliðaár river, but the rest had escaped.

"When the good children of better folk go out in the evenings before bedtime," said the organist, "and steal fifty minks to amuse themselves, or a few crates of spare parts for mechanical excavators, or the telephone wires to Mosfell District, that is just as logical a reaction against their environment as the actions of my two friends – and just as innocent. It is impossible to escape the fact that an object which lies in salt water will absorb salt. The thievery which really matters, on the other hand, takes place elsewhere. You asked whether I wanted to have everything in the country stolen; now I shall tell you a secret: everything in

the country *is* being stolen. And soon the country itself will
be stolen."

I was still standing with my gloves on in the middle of the
room, gaping.

"What will happen to the poor child?" I asked.

"Nothing at all, fortunately," said the organist, and laughed.
"Unless of course the Chief of Police phones up his daddy and
they chat about the younger generation for a while and laugh
and then fix up the next bridge night."

"Worse luck," said the unselfconscious policeman. "Brats like
that should be publicly thrashed at Austurvöllur."*

The organist laughed, amiably and sympathetically, but
thought this observation too naive to answer.

Then the selfconscious policeman uttered his first words and
addressed his colleague: "Have I not often told you that they
indoctrinate you with whatever sense of justice it suits them best
for you to have? You have a petit-bourgeois sense of justice."

I was going to say something more, but the organist came
over to me and put his arm around me and walked me out of
the kitchen into the living room, closed the door behind us,
and made me sit down at the harmonium.

When the half hour was up and the organist opened the
door to the kitchen again, the selfconscious policeman was still
sitting there reading a book, but the unselfconscious one had
gone home.

"I'm sorry," he said. "I couldn't be bothered going home to
my suitcase. But now I'm on my way."

His teeth were whole, and when he smiled he looked posi-
tively childlike, but before you knew it he started frowning again
and began to peer at everything in that stealthy way which
makes a girl say to herself and mean perhaps something rather
special: "He's different from the others." Yet somehow I had
the impression that I knew him. Did he know me?

---

*The garden square in the middle of the administrative centre of Reykjavík,
in front of Parliament House; a favourite spot for strollers.

"Stay as long as you like," said the organist. "I'm going to make some more coffee now."

"No more coffee for the time being," said the selfconscious policeman. "I'm off now. It's quite true what you said: there is no sense in being a petty thief, that's only a pastime for children – and for wretches who go on being children after they have grown up."

"The only conclusion not to be drawn from this fact is that one ought therefore to become a legal thief," said the organist.

"Ah well. I'm on my way."

I accompanied him out. We were going in the same direction. He was no good at starting a conversation, and I did not know what to say either. Our silence was like a fire glowing under a spit; until he said, "Do you recognise me?" and I replied, "Yes, but I don't know who you are."

"I know you," he said.

"Have you seen me before?" I asked, and he said that he had. Then I said, "The difference is that I know you but haven't seen you before."

"Of course you've seen me," he said. "I was one of the men who threw the corpse into your hall the other night."

"Oh yes, now I remember," I said, but it was not so much this that I remembered; rather I was meaning some indefinable secret relationship between us which lay much deeper, an acquaintanceship which it would not be proper to put into words. So I veered away from that subject and started discussing the other: "Don't you think it strange to have everything – youth, good looks, health, education, intelligence and money – and yet to go out like Arngrímur Árland and be carried home in a paralysis of poison?"

"So-called daddy's boys," he said, "the sons of men who have cheated the populace of vast wealth – they know by instinct that they are born receivers. What are such boys to do? They have no vocation to become criminals, and no necessity to become anything else, so they go out to eat and drink poison. That is their philosophy."

"Where are you from?" I asked.

"From the north," he said. "From Húnavatn County, where all the best thieves and murderers in the country come from."

"Really?" I said. "Then we both own everything on the other side of Holtavörðuheiði moor; I am from the north too, you see."

"But have you a vocation?" he asked.

"A vocation?" I said. "What's that?"

"Have you not read in the papers that country people have to have a vocation?" he asked. "The papers are always saying so."

"I was taught never to believe a single word which is written in the papers, and nothing except what is written in the Icelandic sagas," I replied.

"I unhitched the hack from the mowing machine at noon one day in the middle of the hay-making," he said. "And went south."

"To do what?"

"It was the vocation," he said. "And now I have stumbled into the misfortune of being taught to play the harmonium – by that man."

"Misfortune?"

"Yes, he sees through the whole swindle," he said. "What am I to do?"

"Aren't you in the police?" I asked.

"That's a minor detail," he said.

"What's the main thing?"

"That's exactly what I'm trying to find out," he said.

"We are just like any other country people in town," I said. "But you who have a vocation . . ."

"Look at Two Hundred Thousand Pliers," he said, "that superannuated alcoholic who could once only screech. Now he has become both pious and the manager of a Thieves' Company for Snorredda in New York. He would have bought a genuine Rolls-Royce if the British had not refused to service such a vehicle for an Icelander; so he had to buy a Cadillac. Why should I be mowing hay which refuses to dry out? Or

chasing up mountains after some wild old ewe? Why can I not
have F.F.F. for Snorredda in New York, like him? We are at
least from the same district. Why can I not build a church in
the north to provoke these sheep farmers? Why can I not
become the leader of a psychical research society? Why don't
the papers print what I have to say about God, and the soul,
and the next world? Why can't I have an atom poet for a
message boy? And a brilliantined god for a storekeeper? I at
least went to grammar school in Akureyri; and he didn't; and
in addition to that I'm a composer."

"I'm sure our organist knows what we all ought to do," I
said.

"That is precisely the misfortune," he said. "What frightens
me most of all is the thought that the same thing will happen
to me as has happened to the two gods: merely from learning
scales from him and drinking coffee afterwards, they have in
barely a year lost their vocations; and if from lifelong habit
they happen to do a burglary somewhere, they bring the money
home to his house and tear it all up, singing, and throw it on
the floor."

"Yes, he is the man I most want to understand," I said. "I
have only been with him a few half-hours, but each time he
gives me a flower. Tell me about him."

"I have barely got through his scales yet," he replied, "and
I have scarcely started on all the coffee. But already I am almost
a ruined man, whatever worse there is to follow. He makes
terrible demands."

"Moral demands?" I asked.

"No," he replied. "You are at liberty to commit every crime
in the world. He regards crime as a tasteless joke, although in
fact he finds bourgeois ideals, everyday ordinary conduct, even
more absurd; and heroism, whether for good or evil, he
acknowledges no more than the Book of the Way. But . . ."

"What sort of demands then?" I asked.

"Briefly, the first demand is that you base poetry on objective psychology and biochemistry; secondly, that you have

followed in detail every development in art since the days of Cubism; and thirdly, that you acknowledge both quarter-tones and discords and moreover can find the point in a drum solo. In this man's presence I feel like some repulsive insect. And yet he can say to an outcast like me, 'Look on my house as if it were your own'."

"You must be more than a little educated yourself," I said, "to be able to understand him. I certainly wouldn't understand him if he started to talk like that. What's a quarter-tone? Or Cubism? Or the Book of the Way?"

After a moment's silence he replied, "You make me talk, and now I have talked too much. It's a sign of weakness."

"But you still haven't told me what you yourself think," I said.

"Of course not," he said. "The reason a man talks is to hide his thoughts."

If this man had a million, I said to myself, and if he were about fifteen years older, then there would not be much difference between him and the Doctor, perhaps none at all – their souls were of the same colour; except that I did not feel weak in the knees from talking to this one as I did with the other. Both of them had in generous measure that Icelandic talent, straight from the sagas, of speaking mockingly of what was nearest to their hearts – this one about his vocation, the other about his children. The boy I lay with for a few nights once, he never said anything. And I never knew what my father was thinking. A man who says what he is thinking is absurd; at least in a woman's eyes.

"May I see your patterned mittens?" I asked.

He let me see his patterned mittens in the light of a street-lamp in the night.

7

AT A CELL-MEETING

Next day I met the girl and the young man in the baker's. The girl gave me a friendly smile, and the boy solemnly raised his hat.

"I want to settle up," I said, and handed over the money for the raffle tickets. "But you will pardon me if I doubt whether the Youth Centre will be built."

"Why not?" said the girl and looked at me a little aggrieved; and I felt that I had been beastly to her by owning to this doubt.

"I don't know," I said, because I did not want to offend her further.

She looked at the young man and said, "You've lived in such a Centre, haven't you?"

"No," he said, "but for three years I spent all my leisure in such a Centre."

"In Russia?" I asked.

"No," he replied. "In the Soviet Union."

Then the girl started to laugh, she thought it so funny that I should have confused Russia and the Soviet Union.

"Russia," he said in explanation, "was the land of the emperors: yon satanic prison of the nations."

I thought it strange that he should say "yon," for I had never heard anyone use it in that way before. So I asked, "Why do you say 'yon'? Are you quoting from a book? Or is it Communist jargon?"

He thought about it and mumbled something to himself, then finally he said, "'Yon?' – as far as I know it's perfectly good grammar: yon young Iceland."

"I'm sorry for picking you up on it," I said. "Tell me more about the Youth Centre."

He had such a clear and spiritual look in his eyes that I asked myself: can such innocent-looking people belong to a cell? He did not know the difference between the spoken word and books, but that was the only false note in what he said.

"In a Youth Centre youth meets in a civilised and organised fashion to enjoy all the different aspects of culture," he said. "There is a swimming pool and a gymnasium, studios for acting and art, a tower for parachutists; rehearsal rooms for orchestras and soloists, general and specialised libraries; a workshop where boys and girls can learn welding, a printing works to teach hand printing as an art, a comprehensive technical college, a laboratory and a botany department, projection rooms, lecture rooms, refreshment rooms, sitting rooms . . ."

"And a room for flirting," I said.

"Of course," said the girl before she had realised it; and the boy stopped short in his list, cleared his throat and looked at her censoriously, and his mouth hardened a little.

"Icelandic youth should not lie in schnapps-spew under the feet of men and dogs," he declaimed. "Icelandic youth should not be nurtured on murder films and pornographic thrillers, Icelandic youth should not live in the streets where it learns to blaspheme, to shriek, and to steal. Icelandic youth . . ."

"One white loaf and a kilo of biscuits," I said.

"You don't believe him," said the girl, and served me sorrowfully. I saw that I had hurt her to the quick with my frivolousness. I paid for what I had bought and was about to leave.

"Perhaps I'll have a few more raffle tickets, come to think of it," I said, before I knew I was saying it; and I felt myself go white the way one does when one embarks on a secret, strictly forbidden affair. And as always in having an affair, the moment one lifts one's foot the step is taken. "There's one thing I would like most of all," I said, and I even got palpitations and laughed unnaturally, "and that is to attend a cell meeting."

There – it was said!

The boy and the girl looked at one another, in twofold seriousness this time, I am almost inclined to say in double-twice solemnity; here was a problem.

At last he said, "You aren't in the Party."

"What party?" I asked.

"The Party," he replied.

"I'm not in any party," I said. "But if I like the cell-meeting I might become a Communist."

Now they both started laughing again, and the girl said, "I've never heard anything like it: if she likes the cell-meeting! This is literally the funniest thing I have ever heard."

I walked out of that baker's an utter fool, not even knowing the reason why until later – until after I had attended a cell-meeting.

For although they had received my request with less than alacrity at first, thinking it complete nonsense, they changed their attitude after I had gone, or perhaps they referred the matter to the Party leadership. Next day the bakery girl took me aside and said she had been deputed to inform me that I might attend. She said I was to come with her the following evening. That night I slept uneasily, troubled by thoughts of the alarming debauchery which my curiosity or congenital depravity was drawing me into. And seldom have I suffered such a disappointment as when I actually attended a cell-meeting; or rather, seldom has anything been such a relief to me.

In a low-ceilinged basement flat some men and women had gathered, most of them rather elderly; they had all come straight from work and had not had time to change their clothes. There were not enough seats for all of them; some stood leaning against the walls, and a few sat on the floor. The youngest child was sick on the floor. And this was the full extent of the debauchery and all the murder.

The business of the meeting was to debate the Central Committee's draft of Party policy for the Town Council elections. There was a long discussion on whether certain marshland in Mosfell District should be turned into arable land or not. Most of them advocated a system of milk transport and milk distribution different from the one then in operation. An old man made a well-ordered speech about the necessity of inserting into the policy declaration a clause about improving the landing facilities for small boats at Reykjavík harbour: it had now come to the point that Reykjavík Corporation was quite literally evicting the little men who did their fishing in tiny inshore-boats here in the bay; the men who provided the inhabitants of the capital with good fresh fish from the bay had no place of their own along the whole length of the sea front controlled by the Corporation. Then the next item on the agenda was dealt with, the question of a Day Nursery. I was sitting with five others on a divan, crushed into a corner, and to my shame I think I fell asleep; at least I cannot remember what decision was reached on the Day Nursery question.

Then a young man asked leave to speak and began to discuss the newspaper; it was the bakery girl's friend. Yet again it had come to the point where the Party had to make a new effort for the paper, appeal to the Party members, collect new subscribers, collect money, find regular backers. Last week it had been mere chance that the paper had not closed down. The Government had ceased to advertise in the paper because the paper had exposed the Government's plan to steal the country from the people and sell it; and for saying that those salesmen, moreover, were then going to freshen up their reputations by exhuming the bones of the Nation's Darling from his grave in Denmark and giving him a tile-hat funeral in Iceland. The wholesalers had stopped advertising in the paper because it had said that they had F.F.F. in New York. The cinemas refused to advertise because the paper had said that Hollywood did not know how to make pictures. In other words, the truth had touched a nerve, the class-enemy feared nothing except the truth; feared lest the people hear the truth. Now once again the working classes had to make some sacrifices for the sake of their paper. The paper was the poor man's cow; if he slaughtered her or let her waste away to death, the family would die. During this speech I woke up again.

And when I saw these penniless worn people, as worn and poor as my own people home in the valley, reach into their pockets for their purses and open them with these worn hands which all at once I felt I could, weeping, have kissed, and then take out that famous widow's mite, some of them even emptying their purses on to the table and those without purses scrawling their names on a list – when I saw this I felt I was utterly and completely in sympathy with these people and would always be so, however dreary the matters they discussed, whether they wanted to reclaim some marshland in Mosfell District or hold on to their country against the tile-hats who wanted to betray it and sell it from under them. So I too scrawled my name on the list and pledged myself to subscribe 10 krónur a month to the paper's funds even though I had never even seen it.

The woman of the house wanted us to have some coffee before we went, but many, including myself, said they were in a hurry to get home; some said they had not even had a wash yet, and anyway it was getting late. The master of the house accompanied me to the door; he was the cell-leader. He said I was welcome to come again the next time, and that I must then stay on for coffee.

And now I had attended a cell-meeting.

ANOTHER MEETING

The Cadillac was parked outside.

I could not remember exactly the name of the smell which met me when I opened the back door, I scarcely even knew whether I liked the smell or not; a smell is good or bad according to its associations in one's mind. This was at least no worse than that of tobacco smoke. Was something on fire?

When I went through the kitchen into the hall to find out what it was, I saw that the door of the master's study was open. The Member of Parliament was sitting there in his room with his feet up on a chair, his back to the door, hunched over some task. He said Hello, without looking, to the person he could hear walking outside in the hall, and continued to concentrate on his work.

"It's only me," said the maid.

"Would you like a cigarette?" he said. "There are some on the table."

"I haven't learned to smoke yet," I said. "But I can smell something. Is this door meant to be open?"

"I opened it to clear the stink of incense. Come in. I am going to show you something you cannot do."

He spoke as usual in that light-hearted, amiable tone, but a little absently; and so help me I did not know whether I ought to dare, even though he told me to. I was, as said before, the maid; and where was Madam? Still, I was no bondwoman, I was a person, I was a free woman.

"Come in and try your hand with this boy," he said.

"Boy?" I said, and before I knew it I was in there and having a look. And was he not sitting there with a round toy mirror, the sort you get at Sauðárkrókur for 10 aurar, with a little black boy on the back (for such articles must surely be manufactured for negroes)? There were a few small pellets loose between the picture and glass, two black, and five or six white, and the problem was to tilt the picture in such a way that the black pellets landed in the boy's eye sockets and the white ones went into his jaws. And this was what my Member of Parliament was toiling over, with a cigarette smouldering in the corner of his mouth and his spectacles on the table.

"I'm afraid I haven't the knack for that," I said. "I'm such a clumsy fool with puzzles."

"Me too," he said, and looked at me with a smile; and handed me the toy; and before I knew it I had begun to have a shot, with him perched on the table to see how it was going. Then I heard some sort of mumbling going on in the next room, some solemn and yet half-stifled sermon, preached to an accompaniment of God-fearing moans like the last words of a dying man: "O ye, my yearning bones, O love, O spiritual maturity, O light." And there was a strange rattling sound in between, as if a sheep were having its throat cut.

"Are there guests in, then?" I asked, looking up in dismay.

"It seems to be the sheep-rot,"* he said. "We shall pay no attention to it."

But after a while the sermon began again, with the moaning and the rattling, and I started to listen.

"Pliers has rid himself of his old demons and come up with something new," said the master. "The next world, to be exact."

"How do you mean, the next world?" I asked.

"A séance," he said.

"And you here?"

"I spew 6 metres," he said. "On with the boy."

"Pliers," I said. "That's a queer name. Excuse me, but is it Two Hundred Thousand Pliers?"

"Yes, the poor fellow. He has this sort of belief in the next world plus vegetarianism, which is at one and the same time the after-effect and the converse of former alcoholism, a kind of binge gone wrong, if I may put it that way. While he was a straightforward drunkard and businessman, newly arrived from the north, he bought two pliers and five anvils for every single Icelander; hairnets, six for each and every person; an unlimited quantity of boiled American water in cans, to use in soups; ten-year-old sardines from Portugal; and enough baking powder to blow up the whole country – but even the Communists don't know that. Finally, he had resolved to buy up all the raisins in the world and import them to Iceland, but by that time he had also lost his voice except that he continually screeched the vowel A. The Snorredda company saved him. We adore idiots. We are hoping that Two Hundred Thousand Pliers can become a Minister. Now he has made contact, as it were, with the Nation's Darling, whom we consigned to a Danish death a hundred years

---

*A contagious lung disease (adenomatosis – mæðiveiki in Icelandic) which killed hundreds of thousands of sheep in Iceland just after the war.

ago. The Nation's Darling wants Pliers to dig up his bones so that we Icelanders of today can become the well-merited laughing stock of history. We are thinking of exhuming him even though it was proved by experts years ago that his bones are lost. The Prime Minister, my brother-in-law, has now joined in the game. And there, look, you have just got the teeth into the boy's jaws. Now I see you can do everything."

And at that moment singing broke out in the next room, albeit rather inferior singing, out of tune like the chanting at a pauper's funeral – a harsh thing to say in one of the greatest houses in the land: "O, sing a new song to the Lord, sing all the earth to God." Then this pitiful singing came to an end. There was a scraping of chairs, the sitters stood up, and the connecting door into Doctor Búi Árland's study was thrown open. In stalked Madam, ennobled in soul by revelations, and a perky well-dressed man so loosely assembled that his limbs flapped when he walked, particularly his arms: this famous man – at last I was getting a sight of him. Between them swayed a lanky man with a thatch of red hair, glassy-eyed, sweating and dishevelled, his necktie pulled to one side. Then came two women who were midway between being common and upper-class, the one in national costume and the other in a black taffeta dress with tassels dangling here and there; both were absolutely rigid with solemnity, both were in a spiritual condition.

And I was sitting in there with the master.

"What's the maid doing in here?" asked Madam.

"She is trying her hand with the boy," said the husband.

"What boy?"

"The black one," he replied. "What news of the dead?"

"We got marvellous confirmation," bleated devout woman number one.

"It was divine," groaned devout woman number two.

Then they both sighed.

"My friend the Darling," said Pliers, "has confirmed in your wife's hearing – and the hearing of these two – what he has so often told me previously during séances with this future world-famous medium down south. Ó-Ólafur, what's your surname again, lad? – Iceland must have her bones. The Icelandic nation needs spiritual maturity and light."

"And love," said the medium. "Don't forget love."

"Listen, friend," said Doctor Búi Árland to Pliers, "do you imagine that the Nation's Darling ever paid any attention to grass-eaters and total abstainers like you, except on that one occasion when he wrote in a poem, 'The cattle-rearing pasture grows on your mother's grave'?"

"The papers shall have it, the radio shall have it, the people shall have it," said Two Hundred Thousand Pliers. "And if you defeat it in Parliament I shall go to Denmark myself and have him dug up at my own expense; I shall moreover buy the bones and keep them myself. Nothing shall come between my bones and his."

"Will someone not take it upon himself to provide that young man with a handkerchief?" said the Doctor, pointing to the medium.

Pliers pulled a silk handkerchief from his breast pocket, blew the medium's nose hurriedly for him and then threw the hand-kerchief into the fireplace; all with these floppy movements like a rubber doll's. The medium sniffed feebly after this oper-ation and said apologetically, "They draw so much strength from me out through my nose, particularly the large spirits; and absolutely especially the Darling . . ."

"I think you should learn to take snuff," said the Doctor, and then offered the petit-bourgeois women cigarettes; but they only stared at him apprehensively. No further hospitality was offered to this half-class in such a house. I went on trying to get the white pellets into the black boy, and was perfectly clearly aware of the loathing which blazed in Madam's body at seeing the maid playing in her husband's room while she, this great woman descended from such great people, was coming from another world, brimming over with everything holy. But her glares left me quite unmoved; for what was there for me to be ashamed of? If I had fled the moment she arrived, that would have been an act of shame, that would have been to accuse oneself without cause.

"Come, friend," said Pliers, and helped the medium to negotiate the open door so that he would not turn into nothing there in the middle of the room. Madam propelled the half-class women through the door as well and bade them farewell graciously, and they continued to bleat and groan in their sentimental falsetto about the wonders of the next world all the way out into the street.

The Member of Parliament, Doctor Búi Árland, suddenly remembered that he had to have a few words in private with his underling; with a start he ran after him out to the Cadillac, where his agent was already behind the wheel, and conferred with him through the open car door.

I had at last managed to get the pellets into the little black boy, and I laid the mirror carefully on the table so that they should not fall out again. But Madam walked into the room as I was leaving, picked up the mirror and shook it, and then flung it aside.

While I was walking upstairs I heard her shouting through the open door to her husband, who was still talking to Two Hundred Thousand Pliers out at the Cadillac: "Búi, I want to talk to you."

8

HE WHO DWELLS IN THE
MOUNTAIN-TOPS, AND MY FATHER

The Nation's Darling, the pride of all Iceland even though he was born in our forgotten valley, my valley, he who was the dearest friend of the nation's heart, the reborn master-smith of this golden language, the resurrector who, by wiping away our blindness, gave us what we had never seen before, the country's beauty,

Icelandic Nature, and who sowed in the breast of posterity the secret sensitivity of the elf instead of heroism and saga, while he himself lived in loneliness and died uncomforted in a far metropolis, overpowered by the apathy of this degenerate nation which he had touched with the wand of life, crushed by the hostility of degraded men towards things concerning the spirit, and culture, and art: again and again I had heard his name bandied about in unlikely places in Reykjavík, and always associated with the most ridiculous matters; first at the singing atom poet's; then, because of the sale of the country, at a cell-meeting; and now here. A country person in the city lets much go in one ear and out the other because he or she fails to understand the connection between things, cannot reconcile unrelated concepts.

"My friend the Darling has confirmed in your wife's hearing . . ."

The household bondwoman, her face hot, pondered these words while she waited in her room for the master and Madam to go upstairs to bed so that she could tidy up the house for the night.

And at the same time another image came to my mind, the one which visits me in every difficulty and is the answer for me to many a question, not because I have ever understood it but most likely because it is so close to my own self, the marrow of my bones, the very substance of my blood: my father. And when I say his image, I do not mean that haggard face which once was full in the cheeks, the stringy body which once was strong, the hand long-ruined by primitive tools, nor the puckered weather-wise eye; I mean rather his spiritual image, the saga, the one thing he acknowledged unreservedly with a sword in place of a scythe, ocean in place of land, a hero in place of a farmer – but yet softened by a century-old modern era, the era of the first volume of *Fjölnir*,* wrapping in silent bear-warmth

*An Icelandic periodical first published in Copenhagen in 1835; Jónas Hallgrímsson (the Nation's Darling) was one of the founders. It was the rallying point of the nationalist and literary renaissance.

the late-born elves who taught us to appreciate buttercup, bird and star. And after having seen the pale necromancers who in that room with its many forgeries of Nature had talked long-windedly about mildewed bones to him who dwells inaccessible in the mountain tops, that fairy person deepest in our own breasts, I was refreshed and comforted by the memory of this rugged image of my origin.

THE WOMAN LIES DOWN ON THE FLOOR

And I was roused from my trance by a strange noise from below, a tear-laden cry, a scream. Was there murder in the house? Or childbirth in the next house? I opened my windows and there was silence all around, windows all dark: so it had to be here in the house. In a flash I was down the two flights of stairs in my stockinged feet, and standing on the bottom step. Both the doors which were open earlier were still ajar, open into the street and open into the study.

"I hate you, hate you, hate you" – there was no trace of human sound in this hoarse screeching, nor in the mixture of inarticulate noises and coarse oaths which accompanied this inverted declaration of love. Then – "I will, I will, I *will* go to America."

In the middle of the floor of the study this beautiful sleek woman lay on her back, her skirt up round her waist, wearing nylon stockings, silk panties and gilt shoes, belabouring the floor with her heels and fists and screaming, her bracelets jingling with the blows and one gilt shoe flying across the room.

Her husband stood at a distance, watching, wearing a surprised and helpless look; yet I suspected he had seen such a performance before and was not particularly amazed. But it would have been more than ordinary discourtesy towards such an excellent wife to behave as if nothing were happening when she went berserk. I say for myself that I stood as if nailed to the spot, dumbfounded at this unbelievable spectacle. When

I had looked on for a while the man straightened himself slowly, walked to the door, and closed it with an apologetic smile. I closed the outside door and then went back up to my room, because it was not yet time to tidy up for the night.

THE SUPPER PARTY

The nice Americans would come when it was nearly midnight; they had stopped leaving their coats in the vestibule, and went straight to the master's study; and if they came across a house-maid in the hall they patted her on the back and brought out cigarettes and chewing gum. Usually they did not stay long. When they left, the Prime Minister would arrive as before, then some more Ministers, the sheep-rot director, some Members of Parliament, wholesalers and judges, the mournful lead-grey man who published the paper saying that we had to sell the country, the bishops, and the oil-processing plant director. They often sat in conclave far into the night, talking in low tones, and went away remarkably sober.

And every time, on the day after these clandestine but digni-fied nocturnal visits by the great at this end of the street, it came about that other visits, public but rather less dignified, were paid at the other end of the street, whatever connection there might be between them: it was the populace paying a call on the Prime Minister. These people's mission was always the same: to deliver addresses and present petitions to him not to sell the country; not to hand over their sovereignty; not to let foreigners build themselves an atom station here for use in an atomic war; Youth Fellowships, schools, the University Citizens' Association, the Road-Sweepers' Association, the Women's Guilds, the Office-Workers' Association, the Artists' Association, the Equestrian Association: "In the name of God our Creator, who has given us a country and who wants us to own it, and which was not taken from anyone, do not sell from us this country which God wants us to own, our country; we beg you, Sir."

There was unrest in the town; people ran from their work in the middle of the day and gathered fearfully in groups or sang "Our Fjord-riven Fatherland"; the most unlikely people hoisted themselves up and made speeches about this one thing:

You can impose on us limitless taxes; you can have companies which add many thousand per cent to the prices of the foreign goods we buy off you; you can buy two pliers and ten anvils a head, and buy Portuguese sardines for all the nation's currency; you can devalue the króna as much as you like when you have managed to make it worthless; you can make us starve; you can make us stop living in houses – our forefathers did not live in houses, only turf hovels, and they were yet men; everything, everything, everything, except only this, this, this: do not hand over the sovereignty which we have battled for seven hundred years to regain, we charge you, Sir, in the name of everything which is sacred to this nation, do not make our young republic the mere appendage to a foreign atom station; only that, only that; and nothing but that.

When such visits were being made at the other end of the street, all the doors in our house were carefully locked and Madam said, "Draw the blinds in the south windows."

One night in the darkest part of winter there was a new development for this house: both foreign and Icelandic guests were asked to a party together. It was not a dinner party but a supper party. The guests arrived about nine, all in evening dress, all men, and were given cocktails while they were making their greetings. As for food, there were tables covered with American sandwiches, tongue, chicken and salads, with all the appropriate wines, followed by delicious desserts. People ate standing. Finally a punch was heated in a bowl, and whisky and gin were served. Hired waitresses did the serving, and expert cooks stood by in the kitchen. The Yanks left early; shortly after they had gone the aristocracy of Iceland began to sing "Fellows Were in Fettle" and "O'er the Icy Sandy Wastes". Around midnight, the waitresses brought word to the kitchen that the guests were beginning to fondle them as they poured out drinks for them. A little later the girls went home and the guests poured their own drinks. As the night wore on people became drunk, and Pliers helped the host to support those who could not shift for themselves, or carry them out into taxis. At the end of the party I was told to clear the table-ware and leftovers, dry the spillings, empty the ashtrays, and open the windows. The only people left by then were the Prime Minister, very drunk in a huddle deep in a chair, and Snorredda's jack of all trades, Pliers, very sober, filling up his glass for him. The host had seated himself in his study with the connecting door open, and was leafing through a foreign magazine.

"Communists!" said the Prime Minister. "Bloody Communists. I love them. I shall kill them."

"Listen, friend," said his brother-in-law from behind the magazine. "You remember we have to get up early and go to a committee meeting tomorrow morning?"

"And we mustn't forget that the nation's independence now depends on Iceland recognising her bones," said Two Hundred Thousand Pliers.

"Cowards! Come on if you dare!" said the Prime Minister.

"All the newspapers must combine over the bones question," said Pliers. "The Communists too. But above all the clergy."

"Why do I want to sell the country?" said the Prime Minister. "Because my conscience tells me to," he said, and here he lifted three fingers of his right hand. "What is Iceland for the Icelanders? Nothing. Only the West matters for the North. We live for the West; we die for the West; one West. Small nation? – dirt. The East shall be wiped out. The dollar shall stand."

"Friend, we mustn't think aloud," said Doctor Búi Árland. "There are people about. If we speak, what we are thinking could be misunderstood; or even understood, which God forbid."

"I want to sell my country!" roared the Prime Minister. "Everything for only this. They can drag me by the hair all through the town . . ."

"Friend," said the Doctor.

"Eat shit!" said the Prime Minister. "Though they flog me publicly at Austurvöllur and kick me to hell out of the Government I shall still sell my country. Even though I have to give my country away for nothing, the dollar shall conquer. I know Stalin's a clever man, but he shall not be a match for the Prime Minister of Iceland."

"And even though the whole nation betrays the Darling he shall still have me for a friend," said Pliers.

"Where's everybody?" said the Prime Minister, suddenly realising that the guests were gone. A little later he overturned the glasses, stood up and braced himself, and it was amazing what he managed; bracing himself was obviously something innate in this little fat man's blood, the last thing which deserted him in this life; in actual truth he was so drunk that there was nothing left of him except his innermost instincts. Pliers supported him out and put his hat on his head and the man went on echoing himself on the way out through the hall and outside door: "I'm the Prime Minister. Stalin's not so clever as I am. The dollar shall stand."

The Doctor, his brother-in-law and colleague in the Snorredda enterprise, accompanied him and Pliers to the door. The party was over. They drove away, and the master looked at me with a smile.

"My brother-in-law is a delightful man," he said, "and likes to make jokes sometimes when he is tipsy. Fortunately we do not have to commit them to memory; nor repeat them if we happen to drop in to a cell-meeting."

He leaned against a door-jamb and looked at me wearily, while his cigarette smoked itself between his fingers; and he had mentioned a cell-meeting – did he then know everything, even that?

"He is really a very honest man," said the Doctor. "At least when he is tipsy. In actual fact, no man is honest when sober; in actual fact, you cannot believe a single word a sober man says. I wish I were drunk myself."

He took off his spectacles and polished them carefully, put them on again, and glanced at his watch. "Bedtime, and long past it," he said.

But he turned on his heel in the middle of the hall on his way up and continued his monologue: "As I was saying, you can always depend on him absolutely. If he swears something to you in confidence when he is sober, and pledges it on his honour, you can be quite sure that he is lying. If he swears it thrice in public on his mother's name, then, quite simply, he means exactly the opposite of what he is swearing. But what he says when he is tipsy he really means, even though he swears it."

I straightened up and asked, "Is he going to sell the country?"

"Are you not indifferent to politics?"

"Yes," I said. "But all of a sudden I thought of my father; and the church. A-And the stream."

"What stream?" he asked in surprise.

"The stream . . ." I was going to say more, but could not. I said no more. I turned away.

"I don't know what you mean," he said, and I felt him looking at me even though I had my back turned to him.

"Hm," he said. "Good night."

THE OATH

The crowds pressed closer and closer to Parliament House, the speeches getting more and more vehement, "Our Fjord-riven Fatherland" being sung ad nauseam, the shouts and cat-calls everywhere: "Does Parliament not dare to answer?"

The Members of Parliament sat in closed session to discuss whether they should hand over Reykjavík or some other bay equally suitable for an atom station for use in an atomic war; and since the matter had not been anything like fully enough discussed, they were at a loss to know what answer to give to the singing parliament out there in the square. Occasional MPs could be seen peeping out of the balcony window with a smile which was meant to appear nonchalant but turned into a forced grimace. Eventually the front doors of the Parliament building were burst open by the pressure of the throng, and people began to stream inside. Then at last the balcony of Parliament House opened and on it appeared a little fat perky man who began to strike an attitude. He waited until the people below had finished singing "Our Fjord-riven Fatherland", and settled his shoulders, fingered the knot of his tie, patted the nape of his neck with his palm, lifted two fingers to his lips, and cleared his throat.

Then he began to speak: "Icelanders," he said, in a deep, calm, national-father voice; and the people fell silent, acknowledging the drama. "Icelanders," he said, repeating this word which is so little in the world and yet so large, and now he lifted three fingers on high over the crowd; then he uttered his oath slowly and firmly, with long pauses between the words:

"I swear – swear – swear: by everything which is and has been sacred to this nation from the beginning: Iceland shall not be sold."

9

BAD NEWS OF THE GODS

The organist and the selfconscious policeman were sitting at the battered old harmonium with some barely legible scrawled notation in front of them, so engrossed that they neither saw nor heard me when I came in; and for half an hour they were unaware that I was sitting behind them. For a long time they struggled their way through some sort of tunelessness, full of weird sounds which recalled the light over the countryside early in the morning before anyone is afoot. In the end, however, I seemed to perceive a melody emerging, but it came from such a distant place, in addition to which its wonders revealed themselves to me in so sudden a flash, that perception struck rather than touched me. And just as I was beginning to get palpitations over a new world, a fantastic and undiscovered world on the other side of usual form, the two had stopped and were on their feet, animated and exalted, with a light in their eyes as if they had composed the music themselves, and they greeted me.

When I began to ask questions, the organist said he did not know if it were safe to trust me with one of the more important secrets in the world, the name of a new genius: was I stupid enough to come face to face with such a problem without missing my foothold in life? And if I were not stupid, was I then intelligent enough to obey this new maestro's call to each individual to deny the world in which we live and take part in creating a new one for the unborn? But when my organist saw how grieved I was at not having his confidence he was sorry for me, patted me on the cheek and kissed me on the forehead: "It was a violin concerto by Roberto Gerhard," he said, and asked me not to be angry, saying that he had just been joking. "He is a Spanish boy in Cambridge, who does not even know music; if there were any vigour left in the Esterhazy family they would beat him. Let us hope he does not get a bigger funeral than Mozart."

He went into the kitchen to see to the coffee, and the self-conscious policeman looked at me searchingly, to see if I had understood anything.

"It's always becoming more and more difficult to live," he said. "Now I've heard this on top of everything else."

At that moment the gods arrived, Brilliantine with those hot, piercing murderer's eyes, and Benjamin drifting through the ether in a trance of pessimism. The organist welcomed them with his usual kindliness, asked them for news of the godhead and the upper regions, and offered them coffee.

They were agitated and brought bad news of themselves: Pliers had thrown them out. "He has taken up with Óli Figure. Figure says, 'Dig up bones.' It's been in all the papers that they are in communication with the Darling."

"By all means let them go digging," said the organist. But the selfconscious policeman asked, "Where is the Cadillac?"

"He has stolen our Cadillac," said the atom poet. "And I revenged myself by smashing with a sledgehammer all the keys on the piano he gave me. I'm going to bellow like a cow. Then I'm going to kill myself."

"I am quite sure you will not commit any such lechery, my friend," said the organist. "Suicide – masturbation multiplied by itself! You who are a god! No, now you must be joking."

"I have seen all the pictures from Buchenwald," said Benjamin. "It is impossible to be a poet any longer. The emotions stand still and will not heed the helm after you have studied the pictures of those emaciated bodies; and those dead gaping mouths. The love life of the trout, the rose glowing on the heath, *dichterliebe*, it's all over. *Fini. Slutt.* Tristram and Isolde are dead. They died in Buchenwald. And the nightingale has lost its voice because we have lost our ears, our ears are dead, our ears died in Buchenwald. And now nothing less than suicide will do any more, the square of onanism."

"But it is always possible to kill someone," said the god Brilliantine.

The other replied, "Yes, if one had an atom bomb. It is both intolerable and unseemly that a divine being like me, Benjamin, should not have an atom bomb while Du Pont has an atom bomb."

"I shall now tell you what you ought to do," said the organist, and placed before him a plate containing a few curled-up pastries and some broken biscuits. "You should compose a ballad about Du Pont and his atom bomb."

"I know what I'm going to do," said the god Brilliantine. "I'm going to divorce my wife and become a success. I'm going to be a political figure. I'm going to become a Minister and swear on oath; and get a decoration."

"You two are slipping," said the organist. "When I first knew you, you were satisfied just to be God; gods."

"Why may we not achieve a little success?" said the god. "Why may we not get a decoration?"

"Petty criminals never get decorations," said the organist. "Only the lackeys of the big ones get that sort of thing. To become a political success a man needs to have a millionaire. And you two have lost your millionaire. A petty thief does not become a Minister; to be a petty thief is the sort of humiliation which can only happen to gods, such as being born in a manger: people pity them, so that their names do not even get into the papers. Go to Sweden for the millionaires and offer your territorial waters, go to America and sell the country; then you will become a Minister, then you will get a decoration."

"I'm ready at any time to offer the Swedes the territorial waters and sell the country to the Yanks," said the god Brilliantine.

"Yes, but it does you not the slightest bit of good if you have lost your millionaire," said the organist.

"So you think I shouldn't bother to divorce my wife?" asked the god.

"Is there any reason for divorcing wives unless they themselves wish it?" asked the organist.

"But at least it will be all right for us to shorten Óli Figure by a head?" said the god.

"It all depends," said the organist. "Have a biscuit."

"He's down south," said the god. "And goes into trances. But we – we have direct contact with the godhead itself. For instance, if I open the Bible I can understand it. Listen, could I stick a couple of half pastries into my pocket for the twins? They love having a lick at a pastry."

"Yes, you are one of the greatest Lutherans of modern times," said the organist. "And a true paterfamilias, like Luther himself."

"And I don't need to do anything but wait until the spirit overtakes me," said the atom poet. "I have never needed to work on my poems. And if I commit suicide, which is perhaps the most beautiful poem in the world, then I shall do it from divine inspiration, because the spirit moves me to."

"Yes, you are the greatest romantic poet of modern times." said the organist.

"But Óli Figure! His nose runs with snot," said the atom poet. "He says, what's more, that he has an immortal soul. But the worst thing of all is that this disgusting jellyfish from down south should now be in the Cadillac."

"So the Figure does not have an immortal soul at all, perhaps?" asked the organist.

They rejected this completely.

"Then I think you should not shorten him by a head," said the organist. "At least, I should think twice before I murdered a man who had no soul. On the other hand it is quite impossible to murder a man who has a soul, for the simple reason that immortality is the essence of the soul: you kill him, but he lives. And now I must ask you to forgive me for having no time to discuss theology with you any more at present; I need to pick a few flowers for my friend, this lovely young country girl here."

THE KEY

In *Njáll's Saga* there is no mention of the soul, nor in *Grettir's Saga* either, still less in *Egill's Saga*, and these three are the greatest of the sagas; and least of all in the *Edda**. My father was never angrier than when he heard talk of the soul; his

---

*A medieval Icelandic collection of Scandinavian heroic and mythological poetry.

doctrine was that we should live as if the soul did not exist.

When we children were little we were forbidden to laugh – out loud; that was wicked. It was of course our duty always to be in a good temper, but all cheerfulness which went beyond moderation was of the devil; there were many maxims in verse on this subject: "Walk gently through the doors of joy." My father was always in a good temper, and no one had a sweeter smile – unless he happened to hear a joke; then his face would stiffen, as if he heard cutting tools being rasped on one another's edges, and he would fall silent and become distant. No one ever saw on his face an expression of anxiety or grief, not even if the wild horses themselves froze to death. My mother loved everything, hoped everything, endured everything; even if misfortune struck the cow, she was silent. If we hurt ourselves, we were forbidden to cry; I never saw weeping until I went to the domestic college: one girl cried because one of her puddings got burned, another cried over poetry, and a third because she saw a mouse. I thought at first they were play-acting but they were not, and then I felt ashamed in the way one feels ashamed for someone whose trousers have fallen down. There was never an occasion on which my father and mother told us children what they were thinking or how they were feeling. Such idle chatter would have been unseemly in our house. One could talk about life in general, and of one's own life so far as it concerned others, at least on the surface. One could talk endlessly about the weather, about the live-stock, or about Nature so far as weather conditions were concerned; for instance, one could talk about dry spells, but not about sunshine. Likewise, one could talk about the sagas, but not criticise them; one could trace ancestries, but never one's own mind: only the mind knows what is nearest the heart, says the *Edda*. If the story were no longer a story, but began to concern oneself alone, one's own self in the deepest sense, then it was wicked to talk; and even more wicked to write. That is the way I was brought up, this is me; no one can get outside of the self.

That is why I am not going to say how it happened or what it was; I can only tell you the external causes until it ceases to be a story.

I knew that he was waiting for me out in the kitchen, like the last time; I could hear him through the wall without listening, and I knew we would be leaving together. Then my half hour was over and I put on my coat and shook hands with my organist and received my flower. And then the other was on his feet and preparing to leave, and we went out. It was just the same as the last time, except that this time he said absolutely nothing. He walked by my side without uttering a single word.

"Say something," I said.

"No," he said. "I am walking home with you because you are from the north. Then I shall leave you."

"Very well, then, friend," I said. "You can be as silent as you like; it gives me nothing but pleasure to listen to you being silent."

Before I knew it he had taken hold of my arm and drawn me close to him and was walking me arm-in-arm; he walked me quickly, perhaps too quickly, but without haste; and silently; he was holding my upper arm and his hand was touching my side, right up against my breast.

"Are you used to walking with a man?" he asked.

"Not one with a vocation," I said.

"Talk as if you were from the north and not from the south," he said.

We walked on and on, until he said bluntly, "You're cross-eyed."

"Is that so, indeed?" I said.

"It's quite true, so help me," he said. "You're cross-eyed."

"Not one-eyed, though," I said.

"It's quite true," he said. "If one looks at you closely, you're cross-eyed. Sometimes I think you're not, but now I'm quite sure you are. Listen, you've no idea how appallingly cross-eyed you can be."

"Only when I'm tired," I said. "On the other hand my eyes are much too wide apart, just like the owl that I am."

"Never in my whole life have I ever seen anything so cross-eyed," he said. "What am I to do?"

He said all this in a gruff monotone which never undulated, but was hot through and through, and something started up in me at hearing him speak; yet I was not afraid because the difference between this one and the other was still locked in my own knees. And when we arrived at my house and I began looking in my handbag, there was no key there; not a trace of a key; and it was past midnight. I had been given keys to both the back door and the front door, and I had never forgotten to take these keys with me when I went out, knowing perfectly well that otherwise I would not get in; and their place was in my handbag; and now of course I had forgotten them, or perhaps lost them; or they had shed their substance and turned into nothing, through miracle or magic. I picked every scrap and tatter out of the handbag, turned it upside down, and searched the lining to see if the keys had crept behind it, but it was no use. I was out on the street.

"Can't you rouse the people?" he asked.

"In this house?" I said. "Certainly not. I would rather spend the night out of doors than make such people open up for me."

"I have a skeleton key," he said. "But certainly I haven't much faith that it would fit these locks."

"Are you mad, man?" I said. "Do you imagine I would enter this house with a skeleton key? No, I'll wait a little. One or other of the family may not be home yet and can let me in."

He looked at me. "I could imagine you'd be in trouble," he said. "You say yes and no to the same thing in the same breath. You had better come home with me."

And that was how it came to pass. And it was not until dawn next morning, when I was leaving him to go home and had put on my coat, that I happened to put my hand in my pocket, and there of course was the key.

He owned nothing except a trunk; the bed, chair, and table came with the room; but the piano was on hire, for he was so far ahead of me in music that he could think of a piano when I could think no further than a harmonium. Everything was in neat order and array. There was a smell of soap. He offered me the chair to sit on, and opened the trunk and brought out a flask of schnapps, just like any other shrewd and provident country person.

"Perhaps you're going to offer me a bite of tobacco too?" I asked.

"Chocolate," he said.

I accepted the chocolate but not the schnapps.

"What else have you got?" I asked.

"Don't be so impatient," he said. "You'll find out soon enough."

LOVE

I could best believe that love was some sort of rubbish thought up by the romantic geniuses who were now going to start bellowing like cows, or even dying; at least, there is no mention of love in *Njáll's Saga*, which is nevertheless better than any romantic literature. I had lived for twenty years with the best people in the land, my father and mother, and never heard love mentioned. This couple begat us children, certainly; but not from love; rather, as an element of the simple life of poor people who have no pastimes. On the other hand I had never heard a cross word pass between them all my life – but is that love? I hardly think so. I think love is a pastime among sterile folk in towns, and takes the place of the simple life.

There was lived in me a special life over which I had no control, except to an insignificant extent, even though I called it me. Whether I was kissed or not kissed, a person's mouth was a kiss, or at least half a kiss. "You are an innocent country lump, closely akin to the awfullest crime," sang the atom poet when he saw me; and he came remarkably close to the truth, for if anything is wicked it is life itself, which goes its own way

in this moist honeycombed vessel called a body. Did I love this
deep-voiced, straight, burning man? I did not know. Or the
other, the one who made my knees go funny? I knew even less.
Why ask? At one level a girl loves all men without differenti-
ating them into individuals; she loves the male. And that can
be a sign that she loves no male.

"You are wonderful," he said.

"That's also what people say who meet in brief accidental
embraces for a midnight hour in the middle of the roaring
stream of life, and never meet again," she replied.

"Perhaps that too is true love," he said.

To walk home alone at night is a disaster, in novels. Some
girls confuse the state of being in love with being lonely, and
think they are the former when in fact they are the latter; in
love with everyone and no one, just because they are without
a man. A girl without a man does not know where she is placed.
A man comes up to her one night as she stands preoccupied
outside a house, and before she knows it she has gone home
with him, where he confides to her everything: nothing. Was
that love? No, she had only thrust a gag into the gaping jaws
of a ravenous beast which was threatening to tear her apart, a
dummy into the mouth of a thirsty unweaned infant: herself.
The man was no more than an implement; and if that was
wrong, then life itself was indeed the poet-singer's awfullest
crime.

Once some surveyors came from the south to survey waterfalls. One of them was wearing an enormous coat, with his
scarf hanging out of his pocket, and he smelled slightly of
drink. She was seventeen then. He kissed her in the parlour
when she brought him coffee. Why did she go to his tent that
night, even though he had whispered it to her? From sheer
curiosity. She was of course hot and sweating and flushed all
day, from having been kissed at the age of seventeen. His tent
was pitched down in the gully beside the stream, and there he
stayed on his own for three nights; and she with him. She never
said a word to him, and how glad she was that he was married,

or else she would perhaps have begun to think about him. Then he left; and as a result of this I first began to think about myself. In reality, he gave me myself, and in return I own him for the rest of my life, despite everything – if I want to.

The other time was a boy I got to know when I was at the domestic college. First he danced with me for a whole evening, then he wrote me a letter, and finally he whistled outside my window. I sneaked out during the night. We had nowhere to go but we went nonetheless, for nothing can thwart a boy and a girl. But there is one thing they do not like – that it should be discovered, that it should be spread around; this is ourselves, this we alone know, here is the point where experience ceases to be a story, where the story has no longer any rights. But by good fortune he had to go south after we had met three times, and from then on everything was quiet and no one was afraid in that dangerous place, the domestic college, where immorality is defined ethically but not chemically.

And that was all I had lived, a girl long fully grown, until the night I lost the key.

10

I AM DISMISSED

While I was filling the cups at the breakfast table, Madam asked me in a cold courtroom voice, bluntly, and without looking at me: "Where were you last night?"

"At a cell-meeting," I replied.

First she gave a little gasp, but quickly controlled the twitching of her mouth; she made a squeezed, high-pitched sound and then said with remarkable calm, although her face had gone white: "Just so, indeed. And what matters were on the agenda there, pray?"

"The Day Nursery," I said.

"What Day Nursery?"

"We need a Day Nursery," I said.

"Who needs a Day Nursery?" she asked.

"I do."

"And who is to build it?" she asked.

"The public," I replied.

"The public!" she said. "And what manner of creature is that, pray?"

It was quite remarkable how icily ironical the blessed woman could be, considering how deeply she felt. But she could conceal her feelings no longer.

"Are you so shameless," she began, "that you can tell me straight to my face that you have been at a cell-meeting; admit it in my own hearing in my own house; announce it at our table, in front of these two innocent children, yes, even go so far as to present Communist demands here at this table, demands that we taxpayers should start subsidising the debauchery of Communists?"

"Come now, my dear," her husband interrupted, smiling. "Who is demanding that? Thank the Lord, we subsidise our own debauchery first of all before we start subsidising the debauchery of others."

"Yes, is that not typical of you bourgeois political cowards always to be ready to side against your own class? To flourish only in an atmosphere of intrigue, in some morass of deceit? But now it is I who say, Here and no further! I and others like me who have given birth to our children according to the laws of God and man, brought them up on moral principles and created for them a model home – the very idea that we should start to pay for the debauchery of those who want to pull down the houses on our children's heads!" – and here Madam rose from her chair, shook her fist in my face so that the bracelets rattled, and said, "No thank you! And get out!"

The little girl looked at her mother open-mouthed and had started to clasp her hands, but the little fat one filled his cheeks with air. The master went on eating his porridge, and puckered up his eyes and raised his eyebrows, the way people do at cards so as not to reveal what sort of hand they are holding.

Where on earth did I think I was? Had I imagined that this house was just a hillock which had come into being in the landscape by accident? That here one could talk about things with the frivolousness of the poor? Had I imagined that in this house talk of cells was some sort of innocent family whimsy, a refrain one has grown accustomed to hum when the mind is blank? If so, I had made a grave mistake. I was thunderstruck. So hopelessly incapable was I of understanding better-class folk that I did not even know how to keep a servile tongue in my head. In a flash there appeared before my mind the difference between the two worlds in which we lived, this woman and I; although I was staying under her roof we were such poles apart from one another that it was only with half justification possible to classify us together as human beings; we were both vertebrates, certainly, even mammals, but there all resemblance ended; any human society of which both of us were members was merely an empty phrase. I asked, with a sort of idiotic grimace, if I was to consider myself no longer employed in this household?

"My dear," said the man to the woman, "I think we shall find ourselves in difficulties. You are about to go to America. Who is going to look after the house for a whole year? You know that our Jóna is more than half away with the Småland-American gods."

"I can get a hundred maids who are not impertinent to me to my face in my own house," she said. "I can get a thousand maids who either have the grace to tell a lie, or at least say nothing, if they have been up to something the night before. This woman has given me nothing but insolence ever since she came into this house, full of some sort of northishness as if she were my superior. I cannot stand her."

After a moment's thought I realised that I had no further obligations in this house and walked up to my room to gather up my few belongings, determined to go out into the cold rather than stay in this place another minute.

I AM ASKED TO STAY ON

Just then footsteps came pounding towards my door, there was a violent knocking and the door burst open simultaneously; the little fat boy stood there breathlessly in the doorway.

"Daddy says you're to stay until he's talked it over with you," he said.

"How nice it is to be such a chubby little daddy's boy," I said and patted him, and then went on with my packing.

I expected him to leave when he had delivered his message, for he had always had little enough to say to me before, except when he sat on a wall with the Prime Minister's children and the other better-class children of the neighbourhood, shouting at me, "Organist, coal-bum, O my blessed countryside!" Now he waited and watched me folding my Sunday dress and laying it topmost on my trunk, until he said in a funny mixture of impudence and wheedling, "Can I come with you to a cell-meeting?"

"You'll get spanked, darling," I said.

"Shut up and lemme come to a cell-meeting," he said. "The damned Communists will never let a chap come."

"You're surely not thinking of becoming a damned Communist, a sweet little dumpling like you?" I said.

He bristled and said, "You've no right to say anything to me while you're here in this house."

"Now I can say both Yes and No in this house, because I'm leaving," I said.

He dug into his pocket and pulled out a few crumpled 100 krónur notes: "If I give you 100 krónur will you let me come to a cell-meeting?"

"Do you think I'm going to make a damned Communist out of such a sweet little dumpling for 100 krónur?"

"For 200?" he said.

I kissed him and he rubbed it off with his hand. But when he had raised his offer to the equivalent of a month's pay for a maid I could no longer restrain myself and said, "Away with you now and think shame on yourself, my poor little thing. I really ought to take down your trousers and spank you. A mite like you, trying to bribe grown-up folk – I should like to know where you've learned that trick, and you with such a wonderful man for a father."

"D'you think my father doesn't offer bribes if he needs to?" said the boy.

I gave him a box on the ears.

"You'll be put in prison," he said.

"And who's still got a bandage on his hand since the day he was slaughtering stolen minks?" I said.

"Are you stupid enough to think that anything will happen to me or my cousin Bubbi?" he said. "We can do anything, and we can even be Communists if the damned Communists would allow it."

"Communists only want to have good boys," I said.

"I want to see everything and try everything," said the boy. "I'm against everything."

And then I took a look at this child. This was a twelve-year-old boy with blue eyes and curly hair. He stared back at me.

"Why do you always shout names at me when I walk down the street?" I asked.

"We're amusing ourselves," he said. "We get bored. We want to be Communists."

Ready to go, I shook my head.

"Daddy says you're to stay. To wait," said the boy.

"What for?" I asked.

"Wait until Mummy leaves," he said.

"Go downstairs and say that I have nothing to wait for," I said.

I was busy for a moment turning the key in the lock of my trunk, for the catch had jammed. When I looked up again the boy was still standing there in the middle of the floor, with that silken hair, still staring at me with those clear blue eyes. He had stuffed the 100 krónur notes back in his pocket and was biting his nails furiously; I had caught him at last in the act his nails bore witness to, always bitten down to the quick.

"Don't go, stay," he said, without threats and without bribes this time, just in a sincere childish way, plaintively and a little shyly.

And now somehow I felt terribly irresolute, suddenly so sorry for the child; I sat down half helplessly on my trunk and took hold of his hands and held them tight to stop him maltreating his nails like that, and pulled him close to me and said, "My poor little boy."

11

THE CHILDREN I ACQUIRED, AND THEIR SOULS

Madam flew with Pliers to America one day, and I had the children: their father bequeathed them to me, rather than fathered them upon me, at dinner that evening, smiling and preoccupied; it was a case of immaculate conception, as in the folk-tale about swallowing the fish.*

"Then from now on you shall be called by your proper names," I said.

"We shall reply by crushing you. We shall break your bones. We shall grind you," said the beautiful daughter in a slow intense voice, savouring the words in her mouth like sweets – Crush, Break, Grind.

"Very well, then," I said, "if you don't want to be called by your own lovely names I shall re-christen you out of my own

---

*A common motif in folk-tales: the barren woman swallows an enchanted fish and becomes pregnant.

head, for I shall never address you in African. Arngrímur shall be called World-glow; Guðný, Fruit-blood; Þórður, Gold-ram; and Jóna's little Christmas-card child shall be called Day-beam; and now come in out of the kitchen, Þórgunnur dear, and eat with the rest of us."

"The child's mother has entrusted me with teaching the child Good," shouted the cook through the doorway.

"I have no intention of teaching her Evil," I said.

"That's something new, then," she said. "If salvation of the soul comes from the north."

Doctor Búi Árland's face lit up on hearing this reply, and he stopped reading his paper.

The cook through the opening: "Does the Doctor and master want to countermand his wife's wishes on the very day she flies away – for the sake of northerners?"

"Hm," said the Doctor. "I happen to be the Member of Parliament for these terrible people in the north: my constituency, you understand, my good woman?"

"Yes, but is it the constituency of the soul, pray, if I may make so bold as to ask the Doctor and master?"

The children's faces lit up, the whole table lit up.

"What says Ugla, who has newly acquired all these children?" said the Doctor, and scratched the nape of his neck, putting on a careworn expression. "Does she think it healthier for the soul to eat in the dining room or in the kitchen?"

"If the soul lives in the stomach . . ." I began, but the cook was quick to interrupt me.

"And that's a lie," she said, "there's no soul which lives in the stomach, the soul which my blessed Saviour suffered for doesn't live in any stomach, so help me; on the other hand Sin has its origins there, for whatever happens below the waist is of the devil. And that's why the mistress of this house and Doctor's lady told me in so many words that this child should receive its nourishment here with me with suitable prayers and thanks in the kitchen, so that this house shall have someone to redeem it in the same way as the righteous in Sodom and Gomorrah."

"Yes, well, I think the soul finds salvation in the dining room,"
I said, "and not in the kitchen."

"There, you see," said the master. "It is no fun having to
adjudicate between Pakistan and Hindustan. The one state is
founded on the thesis that the salvation of the soul started with
the Hijra, on the day on which Muhammad departed from
Makkah; the other state claims that the soul cannot be saved
unless we transmigrate at least into a bull, if not as ass or even
all the way down to a fish. Such problems can be solved in no
other way than by each person getting hold of a dagger. As far
as I can see, my dear Jóna, we shall just have to equip ourselves
with daggers."

The cook's foster-child had adopted the habit, in order to
counterbalance all the preaching, of missing no opportunity
of cursing and swearing when the woman was not looking. I
had sometimes been astonished at how long the child could
sit in our lavatory behind the kitchen; she would be muttering
something there in undertones for hours at a time. I thought
at first that it was prayers, but when I applied my ear I discovered that she was, as far as I could hear, stringing together
swear words. The poor thing, she only knew some three or
four oaths, really, in addition to a few words for various tabooed
parts of the body; these she had managed to discover by some
unknown means. And when the darling little saint had cursed
everything to hell and back again in private on the seat for a
good half hour she felt much better and came out uplifted,
and began to tend her piddle dolls. After a while she began
to take advantage of the cook's dullness of hearing; she would
sit in the corner of the kitchen with clasped hands watching
her foster-mother at work, and move her lips constantly as if
she were reciting prayers, while in fact she was striving to say
hell and arsehole a hundred times in the one breath.
Sometimes she would raise her voice a little, just to see how
far she could go without the Saviour's agent suspecting any
wickedness.

MURDER, MURDER

The master continued to have the problems of the nation and other countries on his conscience, and for that reason he was always absent even when he was present, a stranger at his family's table – or was he merely bored? He left when the meal was over. World-glow, whom I had so christened because he was the son of all the darkness which existed in the world, was away with his friends somewhere. Gold-ram had gone out to jeer at strangers with his cousins, the Prime Minister's children, down the street, or perhaps to examine locks for fun for an hour before bedtime. And the maiden Fruit-blood swayed silently through the open doorways like a river trout. There was prayer recitation going on in the cook's place when I went up to my room.

And when I was upstairs, and by myself, I suddenly became so alone in all the world that I started thinking that I must be in love; and not merely in love, but literally unhappy, a manless maiden, tortured by the sort of love-sorrow which one thinks there can be no word for except in Danish, but which it is possible to establish and analyse with a simple urine test. I felt within myself all the strange humours which can rage within a woman, felt how this my own body was stirred by the enlarged and intensified presence of the soul, with the soul which was once merely a theological abstraction becoming a component of the body, and life becoming a strange greedy joy bordering on unhappiness as if one were wanting to eat and vomit at the same time; and not only could I see a difference every day in how I was swelling up, but there was also a taste in my mouth which I could not recognise, a glint in my eyes and a colour on my skin as in someone who has had a couple of drinks, a slackness around the mouth and puffiness of the face which suspicion and anxiety magnified for me when I looked at myself in the mirror: the woman who swallowed the trout. Catching my breath, and with palpitating heart, I stared at myself in the mirror. Some moments have the colour of dreams of extreme peril, but this was not a dream: I had awoken halfway up a beetling precipice. Would the rope hold?

So I fell to tramping the harmonium, tramping and tramping with all the ignorance with which a country person can tramp in the hope of being able to hear yet again the echo which was in life before; until I was tired; and fell asleep; and slept for a long time, it seemed, until I woke up to a clamour.

There was a pounding on the door and shrieks; weeping; and my name being called over and over again, and then, "Murder, murder!"

It was the first time I had ever heard the word 'murder' used in earnest, and I was panic-striken.

But it was only those blessed children of mine whom I had just acquired.

"What's all that noise?" I said.

"He's going to shoot me," came a wail from outside. "He's a murderer."

I jumped out of bed in my nightdress and opened the door. There stood my Gold-ram with genuine terror in his eyes, and both hands raised above his head as in American films when people are being killed. Down on the stairs stood World-glow with a revolver in each hand, calmly sighting at his brother. I think, to tell the truth, that I swore. World-glow apologised and said, "I'm getting tired of fellows like him."

"Is there any need to shoot them?" I said.

"They stole revolvers," he said. "I have decided to shoot them with the revolvers they stole."

"I was in bed and asleep," sobbed Gold-ram. "And knew nothing before he came home drunk and stole my revolvers, and was going to murder me. I've never tried to murder him."

I walked to the stairs towards the revolver barrels, right up to the intending murderer, and said, "I know perfectly well you're not going to shoot that child."

"Child?" said the philosopher, and stopped pointing the revolvers at his brother. "He's in his thirteenth year. I had long since stopped getting pleasure out of stealing at his age."

I went for him and wrested the weapons from him. He did not offer any real resistance, but dived into his pocket for a cigarette as soon as his hands were free. He was spent with liquor, and sat down on the stairs and started to smoke.

"When I was nine," he said, "I stole half of all the spare parts for mechanical excavators which the Agricultural Society of Iceland managed to import that year. Let others beat that. And then – finished. A fellow who carries on stealing when he is grown up suffers from a disease we call in pyschology infantilism: Immanuel Kant, Charles XII. Their glands are stopped up. I was going after girls when I was twelve."

"Give me my guns," said Gold-ram, no longer frightened.

"Where did you get hold of these guns?" I asked.

"None of your business," he said. "Give me them."

"Are you being cheeky, my lad?" I said. "Have I just saved your life or have I not just saved your life?"

World-glow had subsided into a forlorn huddle, with the cigarette smouldering between his lips and the whites of his eyes just showing; in his father's house of plenty he was a living portrait of the despair of the times, a homeless refugee in a hopeless situation.

It was finally agreed that the brothers should go to bed and that I should keep the guns in my room; the elder one, however, sat on the stairs for a good while yet, smoking gloomily; I did not hear him reply when I bade him good night. I went to bed and switched out the light. But just when I was drifting into unconsciousness again my door was suddenly opened before I was aware of it, and someone sat down beside me and began to fumble with me. I quickly pressed the light switch above the headboard, and who should it be but this young philosopher?

"What are you doing here, boy?" I said.

"I'm going to sleep with you," he said, and took off his jacket.

"Are you mad, child, taking your jacket off in here?" I said. "Put it on again at once."

"I am neither a child nor a boy," he said. "I want to sleep with you."

"Yes, but you're a philosopher," I said. "Philosophers don't sleep with people."

"This isn't a world to philosophise about," he said, "so the next step is to abandon philosophy. The only thing I know is that you attacked me just now and I felt you; so the next step is to sleep with you. Let me into bed."

"That's not the way to go about it if a man wants to sleep with a woman," I said.

"How then?" he asked.

"There, you see, my lad," I said. "You don't even know how."

"I'm none of your lad," he said. "And I shall sleep with you if I like; if not willingly, then forcibly."

"All right, my dear," I said. "But you overlook the fact that I'm strong."

It was taking me all my time to ward off his fumblings.

"I'm not your dear," he said. "I'm a man. I've slept hundreds of times with every damned thing there is. Aren't you in love with me at all?"

"I was once in love with you," I said. "It was my first night in this house. The police threw you into the hall. You were dead; stone dead; yes, absolutely wonderfully dead; a dead unweaned infant, and your soul with God, quite certainly. Next day you had come to life; and your face had once again tightened up in that horrible way which makes death beautiful by comparison. But now you aren't drunk enough. Drink some more. Drink until you are utterly helpless and don't even know of it when you are rolled through a puddle. Then I shall fall in love with you again. Then I shall do everything that is best for you: carry you to your room, wash you; perhaps even put you to bed completely, even though I didn't dare do that once; but quite certainly tuck you in."

12

THE MAIDEN FRUIT-BLOOD

The maiden Fruit-blood often stared at me in a trance until I began to feel afraid; sometimes I seemed to see refracted in her eyes all the life which exists in plants from the time that a little seed manages to germinate despite all the accumulated disadvantages of Iceland and Greenland, right up to the point where the god starts looking at you with those burning lustful murderer's eyes of his from the deep. Sometimes I would stamp my foot and say curtly, "Why are you staring like that, child?" But she would go on staring and chewing her chewing gum slowly and calmly. Sometimes she would start gliding through the rooms with a cigarette smouldering in a long holder, just like a movie star. Sometimes she would flip through her lessons with a great deal of smoking and chewing, or scribble a composition in enormous vertical lettering, and the scratching of the pen could be heard a long way away like canvas being torn; but soon she would be back into some American light reading with a cover picture of a masked murderer with a blood-stained knife and a terrified bare-thighed girl with high insteps and slender ankles wearing stiletto heels; or start leafing through the pile of fashion magazines which arrived for the mother and daughter from all over the world every week and sometimes every day. A young sprig of a tree, nothing but springiness and sap, a mirage in female form, a parlour-reared Naiad-shape; and I, this lump from the far valleys; was it any wonder that I sometimes felt uneasy in her presence?

I cannot forget the first morning I went in to her with coffee, and stood in front of the bed in which she lay sleeping.

"Good morning," I said.

She woke up and opened her eyes and looked at me from out of another world.

"Good morning," I said again.

She looked at me for a long time in silence, but when I was just about to say it for the third time she sprang up and interrupted me hysterically – "No, don't say it, don't say it. Oh, don't say it, I beg of you."

"May one not wish you good morning?" I asked.

"No," she said. "I can't bear it. They are the two most disgusting and horrible and frantic words I have ever heard in my whole life. Will you never, never say it?"

Next morning I laid the coffee silently on her bedside table and was going out again. But then she flung aside the eiderdown, sprang out of bed and ran after me, and fastened her nails into me.

"Why don't you say it?" she demanded.

"Say what?" I asked.

"Good morning," she said. "I'm yearning to hear you say it."

One day when I was going about my work she had laid aside her lessons before I knew it and had started gazing at me. All at once she stood up, came right over to me, fastened her nails into me, and said, "Say something."

I asked, "What?"

She went on pinching me slowly and calmly, digging her nails in and gazing at me with a smile, watching carefully to see how I was standing the pain.

"Shall I crush you?" she asked.

"Try it," I said.

"Let me kill you."

"Go ahead."

"I love you," she said.

"I thought that was something girls never said to one another," I said.

"I could eat you."

"You would soon have your fill of that."

"Isn't it hurting you at all, then?" she said, and stopped smiling, losing interest.

"A little," I replied. "Not much."

Her interest revived at that, and she dug her dark-painted nails yet deeper into my arm and said, "How does that hurt? Oh, tell me how it hurts."

I think that in the beginning she had considered me an animal in the same way I had thought her a plant. The plant wanted to know how the animal felt pain. On the other hand, I was never aware of any dislike from her towards me; naturally, she thought it ridiculous that a great clod-hopper should drag so vulgar an object as a harmonium into a civilised house and start pounding out on it the children's exercises which she herself had learned at the age of four, before she could even read; but she bore no more ill will towards a north country girl than a tulip does towards a cow.

Another day: she came over to me when I was in the middle of my bondwoman work, put her arms around me, nestled up close to me, bit me, and said, "Damn you"; and then walked away.

Yet another day: when she had been silently scrutinising me for a long time she said, right out of the blue, "What are you thinking about?"

I said, "Nothing."

"Tell me, won't you tell me? I beg you to."

But I felt that the gulf between us was so deep and so broad that even though I had been thinking something, and even if it had been something innocent, I would not have told her it.

"I was thinking of a brown sheep," I said.

"You're lying," she said.

"Well, well. It's a good thing someone knows better than I myself do what I'm thinking."

"I know all right," she said.

"What?"

"You were thinking about him," she said.

"Whom?"

"The one you sleep with."

"And what if I don't sleep with anyone?" I asked.

"Then you were thinking of the other thing," she said.

"What other thing?"

"That soon you will die," said the girl.

"Thanks very much," I said. "So now I know. I didn't know it before."

"Yes, so now you know." She slammed shut the book she had been reading, stood up, and sat down at the piano and began to play one of those heart-rendingly lovely soulful mazurkas by Chopin. But only the beginning; when least expected she dashed headlong into some demented jazz.

13

ORGY

The master of the house, too, had flown off for a while with that soft, fragrant, yellow creaking briefcase of his, and I was left with the children. And as soon as his presence ceased to be felt, the house ceased to be a house and became a public square. First came the children's friends, the accepted ones and the secret ones, then the friends of the children's friends, and then *their* friends; and with that, the whole of Hafnarstræti.* A case of liquor stood in the hall; I had no idea who had paid for it. Some of the guests had brought musical instruments with them, and a female was dancing on the grand piano. About midnight, food was delivered on platters from a deli-catessen store; I had no idea who paid for that either. But at least the domestic staff were not expected to wait on them, the guests served themselves; indeed, the female sinner Jóna had long since retired to her bed, and through those leather

*Harbour Street.

eardrums no discord other than the voice of conscience could ever penetrate. I roamed through the house, keeping in the background.

I imagine that this was to have been a dance, but it was only very half-heartedly that a couple or two trailed on to the floor to jitterbug for a while; on the other hand there was much singing of "Fellows Were in Fettle" and "O'er the Icy Sandy Wastes", but more especially, and in particular, they vied with one another to produce the weirdest sounds without words imaginable; never in my life had I heard in one single night such a medley of inarticulate human sounds. Then came the vomiting, first in the bathrooms, then on the stairs and in the passageways, and finally on the carpets and over the furniture and into the musical instruments. It was as if everyone were engaged to everybody else, couples were slobbering over one another indiscriminately; but I think that no one was in fact engaged to anyone, and that the kissing was just a variation of jitterbugging – with the exception of the maiden Fruit-blood who, in an ecstasy, with childish movements in her body, clung on to a lanky American-looking guy at least twice her age and already going bald, and finally disappeared with this rascal into her room and locked it from the inside.

I had not the physical strength, much less the moral courage, to interfere with any of it; this was just life in a new image, and perhaps not so very new at that, although it was new to me; but when the time was nearing three in the morning I began to wonder how my little Gold-ram would be behaving himself in all this; would he now be out in the dark busy stealing minks and revolvers or perhaps telephone wires to Mosfell District, the little darling? I opened the door of the brothers' room and peeped in. There on the elder brother's bed a sozzled couple lay slobbering, and on the younger boy's bed a girl in a vomit-smeared brocade dress had been laid out in a Christian attitude, with arms folded across her breast. The radio was tuned to some American stud-station, with hideous squealings and rending farts. Then I saw that the door of the clothes cupboard was ajar, with the light on inside; and what was going on in there in the midst of the orgy of the century? Two boys playing chess. They sat facing one another, crouched over a chess-board in the cupboard, infinitely remote from everything going on just beside them: the mink and revolver thieves, Gold-ram and his cousin. They made no reply even though I spoke to them, and never looked up even though I stood at the cupboard door for a long time watching them. And at this sight I was once again captivated by the essential security of life, by the radiance of the mind and the healing powers of the heart, which no accident can destroy. I contemplated once more the civilised peace of the chess game amid the din from the American radio station and the four gramophones scattered throughout the house, some saxophones, and a drum: then I went up to my room, locked the door, went to bed and fell asleep.

LÍNGÓ

Next morning, of course, it fell to me to wipe up the vomit, clear away the broken crystal and porcelain, and remove the alcohol stains and food marks from the carpets and furniture; and I was wondering how many nights like that one it would take to lay a house waste; and I was busy with this all day long until the children began to straggle home from their various schools. All at once I heard goings-on in the vestibule, and when I went to look, the whole thing was starting up again, as far as I could see; a few fair-haired jazz-fiends of secondary school age were drinking Black Death from the bottle and singing "Fellows Were in Fettle" and vomiting in front of the maiden Fruit-blood out in the hall. They were obviously in love with the girl and wanted to show her that they were men, well deserving of a maiden's love. She sat on the stairs smoking a cigarette in the long holder, a little tired, and gave them a cold bewitching smile.

I barged out and said, "This time I refuse to clean up any more spew today, and will these boys kindly remove themselves?"

Of course these bright-haired drink-wan youths poured over me all those insults and obscenities which can only stream out of the well-bred children of better-class people, including such far-fetched vituperations as "double-minus-person", "gas oven fodder", and "Polish-Jew chain-harlot"; but out they stumbled backwards in the end, the poor things, taking their Black Death with them. And I slammed home the lock.

When they had left, Fruit-blood walked over to me, almost right into me as if she intended to force me to give ground, and stared at me with loathing in her eyes like a gangster's moll in a film.

"How dare you throw my men out of my house?" she said.

"Men? Those dirty little hooligans?" I said, and let her come as close up to me as she liked.

"I forbid you to call south country people names," she said.

She stuck her cigarette holder into her mouth and swept grandly away with exaggerated gestures of her arms, wiggling that shapely little bottom of hers regally as she withdrew, then sank down into a deep chair, leant back limply, closed her eyes and smoked with infinite weariness – all pure cinema.

"Ugla," she said. "Come here. Talk to me. Sit down."

When I had sat down she stared dreamily into the blue for a while, and then said, "Isn't he wonderful?"

"Who?" I asked.

"Isn't he marvellous?"

I said I did not know what she was talking about.

"Heavenly," she said.

"Is it a man?" I asked.

"Do you think it's a dog?" she said.

"I don't know,"

"Who should it be but that damned Língó?" she said. "My Língó – don't you think he's a great guy? I love him. I could kill him."

"You don't mean that lanky devil, bald and I don't know what else?"

"Yes," she said. "That's the one I mean. Worse luck. I know he's terribly tall; and going bald; and, what's more, married. But I sleep with him all the same; sleep, slept, having slept; will sleep."

"Are you mad, child? Do you think you can sleep with people at your age? He can be put in jail for that."

"I'm my own boss, my girl," she said.

"That sort of thing never even occurred to me when I was at confirmation age," I said.

"Listen," she whispered. "Have you heard that girls stop growing if they lie with men too early?"

"I don't know," I replied. "But I do know this, that you are such a child, Fruit-blood, that the next time I see that lanky devil I shall give him a good hiding."

BUYING AN ANEMONE

"If everything starts again tonight, the house filling up with people breaking still more crystal and vomiting on the carpets and ruining the veneer of the furniture, what am I to do? Call the police?"

"Why ask me, my dear?" said the organist.

"I don't know what to do," I said.

"In my house criminals and policemen sit at the same table," he said. "And sometimes clergymen, what's more."

"It shocks me to see these drunken young devils," I said.

"Speak not ill of the young in my hearing," he said, unaccountably switching to the formal mode of address, and completely serious. After a little thought he went on: "I imagined there was enough crystal in the world for those who read crystal balls. I for my own part take greater pleasure in a film of ice over a clear brook on an autumn morning."

"But what is one to do when those around one behave both wrongly and badly?" I asked.

"Behaviouristically wrongly?" he asked. "Biochemically badly?"

"Morally wrongly and badly," I said.

"Morals do not enter into it," he said. "And there is no such thing as morality – only varyingly expedient conventions. What to one race is crime, is virtue to another; crime in one era is virtue in another; even a crime in one class of society is at the same time and in the same society virtue in another class. The Dobuans in Dobu have only one moral law, and that is to hate one another: hate one another in the same way European nations used to do before the concept of nationalism became obsolete and East and West were substituted in its place. Among them, each individual is duty bound to hate the other as West is duty bound to hate East, among us. The only thing which saves the poor Dobuans is that they do not have such good weapons of destruction as Du Pont; nor Christianity, like the Pope."

"Are drunk as well as sober criminals to be allowed free rein, then?" I asked.

"We live in a rather inexpedient social system," he said. "The Dobuans are pretty close to us. But there is one consolation, and that is that mankind can never outgrow the necessity to live in an expedient social system. It makes no difference whether people are called good or bad; we are all here; now; there is only one world in existence, and in it there prevail either expedient or inexpedient conditions for those who are alive."

"Can I then come barging in here blind drunk and shoot your flowers?" I asked.

"Go ahead," he said, and laughed.

"Would that be right?" I asked.

"Alcohol produces certain chemical reactions in the living body and alters the functioning of the nervous system: you might fall downstairs. Jónas Hallgrímsson fell downstairs; some people think that thereby Iceland lost her finest poems – those which he had not yet composed."

"Of course he drank too much," I said.

"Do we think it makes much difference whether or not it was morally wrong of the man to take a drink so often? Perhaps he would not have fallen if he had only had ten drinks. Perhaps it was just the eleventh drink which felled him. Is it not just about as wrong morally to drink one drink too many as to remain out of doors for five minutes too long in the cold? You might catch pneumonia. But both are inexpedient."

I went on contemplating this man.

"On the other hand it would deeply offend my aesthetic sense to see a beautiful north country girl drunk," he added. "But aesthetics and morality have nothing in common: no one gets to Heaven by being beautiful. The authors of the New Testament had no appreciation of beauty. On the other hand Muhammad said: 'If you have two aurar, buy yourself bread with the one and an anemone with the other.' Anyone is at liberty to break my crystal. And though my own rule is no drink, it is not a moral rule. On the other hand, I buy anemones."

After a moment's thought I began again: "Do you contend that it is right for a fourteen-year-old girl to shut herself in with a married man and perhaps come out again pregnant?"

He always gave sort of a titter when he thought something funny. "Did you say fourteen, my good girl?" he said. "Twice times seven: it is a downright twice sacred number. But now I shall tell you about another creature which also counts in this case, except that it counts up to sixteen; it is a species of cactus which is said to grow in Spain. There the blessed plant stands, in those scorching Castilian uplands, and counts and counts with precision and care, yes, I am probably safe in saying with actual moral fervour, until sixteen years are up; and then it blooms. Not until sixteen years have passed does it dare to bear this feeble red blossom which is dead tomorrow."

"Yes, but a child is a child," I said stubbornly; and to tell the truth I was becoming a little annoyed at having so frivolous an organist.

"Just so," he said. "A child is a child. And later the child stops being a child – without arithmetic. Nature asserts itself."

"I am from the country, and year-old ewe-lambs are never put to the ram."

"The lambs of year-old ewe-lambs are not usually much good for slaughtering," he said. "If mankind were reared for the slaughter house, to be sold by the pound, your point of view would be valid. It is a common saying in Iceland that the children of children are fortune's favourites."

"Is one then to believe every damned stupid proverb there is?" I said, and was now a little angry.

"Look at me," he said. "Here you see one of fortune's favourites."

It was the same as always: all conventional thinking turned into crude exaggeration, and universally accepted notions into vulgarity, when one was talking to this man. My tongue tied itself in knots, for I felt that anything further I said in this direction was bound to cause him unpardonable offence – this person who had the clearest and gentlest eyes of any man.

"Was it wrong that I should come into being? That my mother should give birth to me the summer after she was confirmed?" he asked. "Was it bad? Was it wicked?"

Something flashed into my mind and I kept silent. He went on watching me. Did he expect me to reply? At last I said in a low voice, the only thing I could say: "You are so far ahead of me that you are almost out of sight; and I hear you as if on the long-distance telephone from the other end of the country."

"She was a clergyman's daughter," he said. "Christianity has robbed her of all peace of soul. For these few decades of a whole lifetime she has lain awake most nights to beg forgiveness of the enemy of human life, the God of the Christians; until Nature now in her mercy has deprived her of memory. You may now be thinking, perhaps, that those who believe in such a bad god must become bad themselves, but that is not so: man is more perfect than God. Although this woman's doctrine, in which she was brought up from childhood, told her that all people were lost sinners, I have never heard her censure any person with so much as half a word. All her life is symbolised in the only words which she knows in her dotage, when she has forgotten all other words: Please do; and, God bless you. I think she has been the poorest woman in Iceland; nevertheless for half a century she has kept open house for all Iceland; and most especially for criminals and harlots."

I was silent for a long time, until I looked up at him and said, "Forgive me." And he patted me on the cheek and kissed me on the forehead.

"I am sure you understand now," he said with an apologetic smile, "why I am always stung if I hear views which reflect on my mother; and on me; on my existence as a living being."

14

ÓLI FIGURE MURDERED

As a result of the Prime Minister's last oaths there was no more discussion for a while about selling the country. There was now to be an interval of a year, followed by Parliamentary elections over the matter, and meanwhile attempts were to be made to get the representative of the Great Power to moderate the wording of the application: to ask not for a base for attack or defence in an atomic war, but rather for a shelter for any welfare missions which might be dispatched to alleviate the sufferings of European races. A temporary truce was declared between street and State. The Communists stopped saying that F.F.F. was going to sell the country, and F.F.F. stopped writing that people had to be true Icelanders and dig up bones. But in the middle of the calm which had fallen over country-sellings and exhumations, the main tidings of Christmas were that Óli Figure was found in a hut down by the sea with his head smashed in; the iron bar with which he had been assaulted lay nearby. As is the custom when murders are committed, little was written about it in the newspapers, so as not to offend the murderer and his family; until someone had the fine idea of blaming the murder on an unknown American negro, for it did not matter in the least if a black Yankee and his family were offended.

PHILOSOPHY FOR THE ADVANCED

When I came home one evening, between Christmas and New Year, there, standing in the hall, was the man who was to me the most unknown of all, the most incomprehensible and the most distant, even though he was closest of all to me in that mysterious disintegrating way which I shall never admit: the father of the children; the husband of the woman; that famous man, my employer.

"Hello."

I replied, "Good evening."

There was no party on, and the house was silent. He had just arrived from the airport, and his leather case stood in the hall.

"Where are the children I gave you?" he said.

I said I hoped they were out enjoying themselves.

"Let us hope so," he said. "People should enjoy themselves while they can, for the time comes when they are bored with enjoying themselves. I would give a lot still to be able to enjoy going to the cinema."

I only wanted to disappear as quickly as I could behind locked doors, for I could never think of anything to say when he spoke to me; I am sure that in my eyes could have been clearly read the palpitation of my heart at his return, once more chatting in that bantering melancholy absent-minded way of his.

"Good night," I said abruptly and without preliminaries, and turned to go.

"Ugla," he said.

"What?"

He inhaled so deeply on his cigarette that no smoke came out. I paused in the doorway.

"These children," he said.

I waited in the doorway and watched him smoke.

"It is said that a man forgives those he understands, but I think that is a fallacy; at least, a man first and foremost forgives those he does not understand, such as children. Now the year is almost at an end and the main juvenile entertainment of the year is approaching – blowing up the police station. My cousin the Chief of Police is always telling me to keep the little boy indoors. Should I bother to do that at all? Anyway, my children have always taken part in blowing up the police station on New Year's Eve. I think it much the simplest thing just to let them blow it up, forgive them, and then build a better police station."

"Forgive me for being so silly," I said, "but – blow up the police station? On New Year's Eve? The children? Why?"

"I don't know," said Doctor Búi Árland. "But it is always possible to think something up: New Year's Eve is the occasion which reminds us most of the impotence of the self in time. Previously, children could conquer God by loving Him and praying; He made them shareholders in omnipotence. Now God has departed, no one knows where – unless something of Him is left in the Småland-American sect. And the children raise a rebellion against the impotence of the self in time."

"But the police station?" I said.

"Perhaps that is one of the symbols," he said, "a symbol the child understands; a symbol of this enemy of the self; a symbol of this disembodied power which says: You have no share in omnipotence. New Year's Eve – time is passing; you are not only impotent in time, but soon there will be no self at all. Do you understand me?"

"No," I said. "I think we need a Youth Centre, that's all."

He smoked and smoked, but no smoke ever appeared, and he puckered up his eyes against the headiness of the tobacco.

"No wonder you do not understand me," he said. "A healthy person does not understand philosophy. But you who do not understand philosophy, tell me this – what is to be done with children? A Youth Centre, you say. Perhaps. Previously, when we understood the god but not the man, there was no difficulty in bringing up children. But now: the god, the only thing we understood, has betrayed us. Man is left by himself, the unknown. Could a Youth Centre help in such a case? I'm sorry for detaining you like this."

"It gives me nothing but pleasure to hear you speak, even though I don't understand you," I said.

"Say something yourself now," he said.

"I haven't anything to say."

"A Youth Centre," he said. "Yes, it could well be. But . . ."

"And now I ask for a Day Nursery," I interrupted, and felt myself suddenly go hot all over.

"Ah yes, I'm afraid we are against Communism," he said, and yawned wearily. "We are not reflex conditioned to it, as they say in psychology; we are conditioned against it and consequently afraid of it. But no one doubts that Communism will win, or at least I know of no one who doubts it – I can confide all this to you because the hour is midnight, and a man becomes loose-tongued then, if not downright frivolous. You, on the other hand, are not conditioned against Communism and you have no occasion to be afraid of it; so for that reason you can be a Communist if you like, it's quite becoming for a healthy country girl from the north to be a Communist – more so, at least, than being a lady. I understand you, even though I myself would rather go to Patagonia."

"Patagonia?" I said. "What's that? Is it an island?"

"Perhaps I should rather come to you," he said: "to the over-shadowed valley, the secret place, as Jón the Learned* put it.

---

*Jón Guðmundsson, a seventeenth-century Icelandic antiquarian; a prolific writer, and deeply superstitious, he wrote a book in 1644 about the "hidden places" and "secret valleys" of Iceland.

Perhaps we shall set up house and keep a ewe and play the harmonium. Good night."

ENJOYABLE NEW YEARS'S EVE

"Well then, now we shall go to a cell-meeting," I said on New Year's Eve, and took Gold-ram with me – to the organist's. Later the boy told me that it had been the most enjoyable New Year's Eve he had ever spent, and that he had never once wanted to blow up the police station all evening. And yet nothing really happened at the organist's except the usual – coffee, cakes and cordiality. The Cadillac was parked outside and the pram stood inside the room. The gods were highly elated and said they had murdered Óli Figure to celebrate Christmas.

"What about the Cadillac?" asked the fat unselfconscious policeman.

"Pliers is in America," they replied. "And we have the keys."

"I'd be surprised if you don't come a cropper over stealing the Cadillac," said the unselfconscious policeman.

The atom poet sang the Greek hillsmen's song "Ammanamma", which was like the howl of an extremely unhappy dog, and Brilliantine accompanied him on the salted fish. Then they sang a dirge they had composed in memory of Óli Figure:

> Óli the Figure is fallen,
> Eclipser of our people,
> The fell fiend of Keflavík:
> He wanted to sell the country,
> He wanted to dig up bones;
> Wet as a jellyfish
> He wanted atom war in Keflavík.
> Óli the Figure is fallen,
> Eclipser of our people,
> The fell fiend of Keflavík.

There was a country pastor sitting in the kitchen playing Ombre with the host and the two policemen; they were all in excellent humour, particularly the pastor, who had been with the gods and got some Black Death from them. When I arrived with the boy they quickly made room for him in the Ombre game, and the fat policeman, who was off duty that New Year's Eve, gave him some snuff from a silver mull, making him sneeze, instead of serving him with tear gas in front of the police station, as he had done the previous year. The old woman went round with water in a cardboard box saying Please do, and patted us on the cheeks and blessed everyone in the world and asked how the weather was. Cleopatra lay on the broken sofa, elegantly dead, with half of her set of false teeth in her lap.

During the dirge for the late Óli Figure the twins woke up, and the god Brilliantine had to take them one on each knee; oh, they were such blessed little darlings, with their dark eyes and that fine chestnut down on their heads; and when I looked at their faces I understood why the old woman loved mankind so unreservedly. They stopped crying when they were perched on a knee, and the god dandled them up and down and sang.

I saw to the coffee entirely, so that the host should not have to interrupt his card game. Over the coffee the gods began to argue about divinity with the country pastor; they demanded that he should light their cigarettes for them and pray to them and preach about them in church on Sundays. The god Brilliantine claimed to be the madonna in male form, the Virgin Mary with penis and twins; and Benjamin said that he had composed the atom poem 'Oh tata bomma, tomba ata mamma, oh tomma at,' which was at one and the same time the beginning of a new Genesis, a new Mosaic Law, a new Corinthian Epistle and the atom bomb.

The pastor, a big thickset man from the west, said that the right thing to do would be to take off his jacket and give them a hiding; the godhead had never manifested itself in fools, he said, and the devil, not he, would light their cigarettes for them: "And might I inquire of the right honourable police officers

how it is that self-confessed murderers are not thrown into
jail?"

The unselfconscious policeman replied, "Committing a
crime is the least of the difficulties, my dear Reverend; it can
be much more difficult to prove that a person has committed
it. The last time these young men were up before a judge they
falsely confessed to twelve other crimes as well, so that the
whole matter had to be gone into afresh and no one has got
to the bottom of it yet."

Eventually the pastor lit their cigarettes for them and was
given more Black Death. The gods asked if any others wanted
some Black Death? A tiny croak was heard from Cleopatra and
she fluttered an eyelid; but then she died again.

"Reverend Jón, hand me Cleopatra's teeth for the girl twin
to play with," said the god Brilliantine. "And can I ask for a
drop more milk for the boy twin?"

Then the town clock struck twelve and the ships hooted in
the harbour. The pastor stood up and went to the battered
organ and played "The year has now passed into the bosom
of time", and we all joined in, and then we wished one another
a happy and prosperous New Year.

15

COLD ON NEW YEAR'S EVE

The boy was not at all put out when he realised that I had
tricked him by taking him to an organist's instead of to a
Communist's. He said, "I'm sure that Communists aren't nearly
as clever as organists; and the organist said I could come back
and solve chess problems with him whenever I liked."

The boy walked beside me in silence for a while and then
said, "Listen, do you think these two madmen have really killed
a man?"

"Far from it," I said. "I think they were just teasing the pastor."

"If they're in contact with God they have every right to kill people," he said. "But I don't think they are in contact with God. I think they're extremely ordinary people, except that they're mad. Don't you think people who say they're in contact with God are mad?"

"That may well be," I replied. "But I also think that people who steal minks and revolvers are a little mad too."

"You're an ass," he said.

It was New Year's Eve, and there were sleet showers. I was triumphant and relieved – or was I perhaps not – at having left without saying a word to that stranger, the policeman from the north; I had not even looked in his direction all night, although I had wished him a Happy New Year for appearances' sake along with the rest of them. I should think not, indeed.

"Let's walk faster," I said to the boy. "I'm cold in this raw weather."

He caught me up at the gate. He must either have run or taken a taxi, for he had stayed behind in the kitchen at the organist's when we left.

"What do you want, man?" I said.

"I never see you," he said.

"To the best of my knowledge you have been looking at me all evening," I said.

"I haven't seen you for nearly two months," he said.

"What does he want?" said the boy. "Shall I call the police?"

"No, dear," I said. "Hurry inside to bed. I'll be right behind you."

When the boy had gone in, the northerner asked, "Why are you angry with me? Have I offended you in any way?"

"Yes and no," I replied.

"Aren't we friends?" he said.

"I don't know," I replied. "It doesn't look like it. And now I'm not standing out here any longer, in the raw cold."

"Come home with me," he said. "Or I'll come with you – upstairs."

"What for?" I said.

"I need to talk to you."

"I should think not, indeed," I said. "First I go home with you one night, because I'm a coward who knows no one, anywhere. I must probably have thought we would become friends. Then a month passes, and another month passes; it doesn't even occur to you to telephone. Finally at long last we meet by accident, and then you think all of a sudden you need to talk to me. What do you need to talk about?"

"I need to talk to you," he said.

"Is it not Cleopatra you mean?" I said.

Then I walked the three or four paces from the gate to the house and opened the door. He followed me. "Wait," he said, when I had crossed the threshold. But he made no attempt to take hold of the door against me, even though I was not holding it very tightly, nor did he stick his foot in the door when I closed it, but was left behind outside. And I walked up to my room a free woman, if such a woman exists.

CINEMA OR SAGA?

The house was asleep – or was there no one at home, perhaps? I opened up the rooms and switched on the lights to see what had to be done for the morning, but there did not seem to have been any party. I was about to go upstairs, when I heard someone come out of a room on the first floor; and suddenly I saw a grand majestic lady come gliding down the stairs towards me. At first I could only distinguish the outlines, a voluminous wide-sleeved fur coat and underneath that a full-length evening-gown; next I saw protruding from under the hem of the gown red-painted nails through open-toed white shoes with platform soles a hand's breadth in thickness. She hugged the fur to her breast with one long white hand agleam with jewels,

and her hair was brushed out across her shoulders in a mixture
of some magnificent coiffure and natural waves; she had
pancake make-up on her face, near-black lips the colour of
dried blood, and a sleep-walker's frozen expression. I literally
felt I was once again watching the mobile cinema at
Sauðárkrókur: this was exactly the woman used in all
Hollywood pictures to beguile country folk and the people in
a hundred thousand little places, this creature who also starred
in all the cinema magazines which are bought in wretched
destitute homes where there is no water closet . . . until
suddenly I saw that this was not a woman, this was a child; it
was none other than Fruit-blood, alone in the house, coming
downstairs to go out in this monstrous outfit, and the time
nearly morning.

"What a sight you are, Fruit-blood, what damned movie star
are you copying, child?" I said. "Are you trying to frighten me?"

She did not look at me, but went on gliding down the stairs
in the same trance, then past me through the hall on her way
out through the vestibule without seeing or hearing. But as
she took hold of the door handle I put my hand over hers:
"Fruit-blood, are you walking in your sleep, child?"

She stared at me with those piercing unearthly cold night-
eyes and said, "Leave me alone. Let me go."

"I can't believe you're going out, child, alone; it's nearly
morning."

"Yes," she said calmly. "I was just coming in. And now I am
going out. I was at a dance. And now I am going to a dance."

"Walking – in that get-up?" I said. "In sleet and slush?"

She stared at me with those eyes in which I could never
distinguish cinema from insanity, and then replied very calmly,
"If you wish to know where I am going, I am going to walk
into the sea."

"Fruit-blood," I said. "What's the point of this tomfoolery?"

"Tomfoolery?" she said. "Do you call it tomfoolery to die?"

She tried to turn the door-handle, but I still held on to her
hand.

"You're not in your right mind, child," I said, still keeping her away from the door. "I'm not letting you go until I've asked your father."

"Ha ha, do you imagine he's at home for festivities?" she said. "In this loathsome house? With these loathsome people?"

"Now you're going to talk to me, Fruit-blood," I said, "and I to you."

"That shall never be," she said, and then tried to compensate for the hollowness of that old saga phrase in her mouth by assaulting me. She beat at me a few times with her clenched fists, not with the knuckles but like a child, with the soft edge of her hands, and then she tried to bite; but I would not let her out. She did not bother to fight me for long; when she saw she was not my match she turned back into the hall, and as she stood there in the middle of the floor after the struggle she let the huge fur sink, as if she were losing hold of it, down off her slight shoulders to the floor, where she let it lie like some sort of discarded magic cloak, and became once more a slimly built girl with awkward, loose-jointed calf movements in her body. Then she huddled herself into a ball in the corner of a sofa so that her knees touched her chin, knuckled her hands into her eyes, and wept – at first with huge convulsions and great sighs, but changing soon into the squealing of a child. Then I realised that this was not all pure play-acting. Or was it such good play-acting?

I tried to approach her as cautiously as I could: "What's wrong? Can nothing be done to make it better? Can't I do something?"

She took her fists from her eyes and waved them about in the air as if she were turning two churns simultaneously, screwed up her face and bawled, "Ah-a-a-ah, I'm pregnant as hell."

"Oh the scoundrels!" I blurted out. "That's just like them!"

"And he didn't dance with me all night, didn't even look at me, and just imagine, what a swine – he went home from the dance with his wife; he could at least have controlled himself over that, he could have spared me that. I didn't think I deserved rudeness from him on top of everything – with his wife, can you imagine it? And me pregnant for six weeks."

"I thank you for telling me this, Fruit-blood," I said. "Now we shall put our heads together."

"I will, I *will* go into the sea," she said. "How is a girl like me to live? The children will hiss at me at school, my mother will kill me in New York, the Prime Minister will sell me to a brothel in Rio de Janeiro and my grandfather would rather lose his fish-oil factory. My father will be jeered at in Parliament and the University, and the people in Snorredda will snigger into the adding machines as he walks past; and the Communists will stage a protest march past the house and say: There's the little pregnant bitch of a Capitalist brat."

"I can swear to you that such a wicked word as you used just now doesn't exist in the whole Communist Party," I said. "It is called in the language of all decent folk to be 'blessedly in the family way'. In your shoes I would go straight to my father, that man of no prejudice."

"Never as long as I live shall I do my father that shame," she said.

"As if he hasn't found a way out of greater difficulties than this!" I said. "Genteel people with morals and delicate nerves send their daughters abroad when they get into trouble, even though uncouth people like us don't understand that sort of thing and just have our children where we are. And now I shall tell you a little story, my girl: I think, you see, that I am pregnant myself."

"Are you telling the truth, Ugla?" said the girl. She sat up on the sofa and embraced me. "Do you swear it on oath? And are you not going to kill yourself?"

"Far from it," I replied. "But the time is coming when I shall have to go north, for my baby's Day Nursery is with Wild-horses Falur of Eystridalur."

She leaned back from me again and said, "I'm sure you're trying to trick me. What's more, you're just trying to comfort me, and that's a hundred thousand times more humiliating than letting oneself be tricked."

"Now I'll tell you, Fruit-blood, what your father will do if you go to him and tell him everything," I said. "He will write out a dollar order for you and send you with the next plane across the Atlantic to your mother. And no one need try to tell me that such a woman does not understand her children. And so you're in America. No one suspects anything, you're in America and you have the child, and afterwards you stay on in America for one, two, three years and finally you come home a reinstated virgin, as we say in the country, and the best match in the whole of Iceland."

"But what about the baby?" she asked.

"After two or three years, when the news gets about, the story will by then be too old for anyone to say anything, and everyone will love the child – yourself most of all. And it's a common saying that the children of children are fortune's favourites."

"Shall I then give up the idea of killing myself?" she asked. "And I who had been so looking forward to returning as a ghost and haunting that swine who went home with his wife!"

"Men don't care in the least if women kill themselves," I said. "If anything, they feel relieved. They are rid of all the fuss."

After some thought she asked, "Don't you think he would then feel that it was he who had killed me?" But she answered herself, "I could best believe he doesn't have a conscience at all. In actual fact, I ought to kill him. What do you think? Shouldn't I attack him, as in the sagas, and kill him this very night?"

"Women never did that in the sagas," I said. "On the other hand, they sometimes got betrothed a second time and then, when opportunity arose, they sent this second lover to an encounter with the former one. It was their custom to make the one they loved the less slay the one they loved the more. But in the sagas things did not happen all in the one day, Fruit-blood."

Eventually, the result of our discussion was that the maiden Fruit-blood neither went out to die on that occasion, nor to murder her lover either, but asked if she could sleep with me up in my room for the rest of the night, because she was slim and shaky in the nerves and I sturdy and from the north.

16

TO AUSTRALIA

The girl slept till late the next day. When she rose she did not bid me Good day, but got dressed up and went to a New Year party. I behaved as if nothing had happened. But I had no idea whether she might not yet run into the sea when least expected, for no one could be certain about that child. In the evening the phone rang; it was her. She talked with a hot palpitating breathlessness as if she had been drinking, in a feverishly rapid torrent: "You mustn't say anything to Daddy. Daddy must never know a thing. I'm going to run away."

"Run away?" I said. "Where to?"

"To Australia," she said. "I'm engaged."

"Congratulations," I said.

"Thanks," she said. "The plane goes at five past midnight."

"And have you nothing to get ready?" I asked.

"No," she said. "Except that I haven't got a toothbrush; and no nightdress either, in fact. But that doesn't matter."

"It is perhaps forward of me to ask to whom you are engaged, Fruit-blood," I said.

"It's an Australian officer, and he's leaving tonight," she replied. "We're going to get married in London tomorrow."

"Hmm, Fruit-blood," I said. "If you'll tell me one single word of sense then I won't tell anyone anything. But if you behave like a lunatic I shall tell everyone everything, and first of all your father. It's my duty. Where are you, child?"

"I can't tell yoú that," she said. "Goodbye. And all the best. And thank you for last night. Though I live to be a hundred thousand years old I shall never forget you for that."

And with these words she hung up.

Some time at the beginning of my stay here it had been impressed on me not to put down the receiver if there were mysterious anonymous phone calls, but to report the fact, so that the connection with the rogue's number should be kept unbroken. I laid the receiver down on the table, beside the telephone, and told the master. I said that Fruit-blood was ill in town and would be glad if he could go to see her: her number was still connected.

In fact, the girl had left the phone when he came into the room, but the number was still connected, and he was careful not to disconnect it.

"Did you say Guðný was ill?" he repeated. "What is wrong with her?"

"She was not very well last night," I replied. "And I think not fully recovered yet."

"Drunk?" he asked bluntly – and without a smile.

"No," I said.

Then he smiled again. "Yes, what does one not ask these days?" he said. "When I was growing up there was in the whole town only one old fishwife who drank. We street-boys were always after her. Now it is considered quite the thing for a better-class citizen of Reykjavík to ask about his newly confirmed daughter: Was she drunk?"

Was he accusing someone? Or excusing? And if so, whom? I was silent. I kept silent, moreover, in the face of all his further questions, except to repeat that the girl was undoubtedly not feeling well and that in his place I would try to trace her.

He stopped smiling again, looked at me searchingly, lifted his eyebrows, took off his spectacles and held them between his fingers, breathed on the lenses and polished them; and there was more than a hint of unsteadiness in his fingers. Then he put his spectacles on again and said, "I thank you."

He put on his coat and hat and went out, saying at the door, "Please let the phone stay connected."

I heard him backing the car out.

MOTHER OF MINE IN THE SHEEP-PEN

That night I went to sleep early; and when I awoke again I thought it must be morning or even broad daylight and that I had slept in, for the master himself stood in the doorway. I started up in bed and said "Huh?", panic-stricken.

"I know it is wicked to wake people in the middle of the night," he said, with that tranquil night-vigil calm which has so uncanny an effect on a person awakening; and went on, "It was as you said, little Guðný was not feeling very well; she is still not feeling very well. I searched until I found her and took her to a friend of mine, a doctor. She will be feeling better soon. You are her confidante. She trusts you. Will you go in to her and sit with her?"

It was 4 a.m.

Her father must have carried her from the car up to her room in his arms, for she was in no condition to walk. She lay on a sofa, pale as death and with her eyes shut, child's face and tangled hair, the dark red wiped from her lips and the colouring from her cheeks. Her father had taken off her shoes but not her coat. She neither moved nor fluttered an eyelash when she heard me enter. I went over to her and sat down beside her and took her hand and said, "Fruit-blood." After a moment she opened her eyes and whispered, "It's all over, Ugla. Daddy made me go to a doctor. It's all over."

"What happened?" I asked.

"He pushed irons up me. He killed me. There were bloody shreds of something in the bowl."

"In the bowl? What bowl?"

"In an enamel bowl."

I took off her clothes, put a nightdress on her and laid her into her bed. She was drained of strength by the drugs, and half-delirious much of the time, moaning in a weak and fluttering voice; but when I thought she was asleep at last she suddenly said out of the blue, opening her eyes and smiling, "Now I too shall hear 'Mother of Mine in the Sheep-pen' sung when I am big."*

"Dearest little Fruit-blood," I said. "I wish I could do something for you."

"I should have gone to Australia," she said.

Then she slipped back into a stupor, far away from me, and the thought fluttered through my mind that she might die; until she said, "Ugla, will you tell me a story about the country?"

"About the country?" I said. "What can you want to hear about the country?"

"Tell me about the lambs . . ."

I saw the girl's eyes begin to twitch with weeping; and then the tears. And anyone who weeps does not die; weeping is a sign of life; weep, and your life is worth something again.

So I started to tell her about the lambs.

17

GIRL AT NIGHT

By the month of Þorri,† a month which does not in fact exist in towns, I had become quite convinced – and indeed much earlier than that. The symptoms all matched; all the things were going on inside me which you read about in books for women, and much more besides, I think. I dreamed about the man all

---

*From the folk-tale about a farm girl who killed her illegitimate baby in a sheep-pen in order to be free to go to a dance. The baby appeared to her mother as a ghost and sang this song to her.

†In the old Icelandic calender, the first month after midwinter, from mid-January to mid-February.

night sometimes, often nightmares, and started up from sleep and had to switch on the light, and could not go to sleep again before I had promised myself to go to him and beg his forgiveness for having shut him out on New Year's Eve; and invite him to provide for me in whatever way he thought best.

But in the mornings, when I awoke, I felt that I did not know this man at all, much less that he concerned me at all, and that the child was mine alone. Then I also felt that, in general, men never owned children at all, but rather that the woman alone owned them as in pictures of Mary with the Child; the Invisible is the father of all children, the man's part in it being purely fortuitous, and I understood well those primitive races which do not associate sexual intercourse with babies. He shall never see my child nor be called its father, I said to myself. Was it not now time that a law was passed forbidding men to call themselves the fathers of children? But when I started thinking more closely about it I felt that the mother did not really own the child either; children owned themselves – and their mother too, in accordance with the law of Nature, but for no longer than they had need of her; owned her while they were growing in her womb, and while they were eating her, or rather drinking her, for their first year. Human society is the one which has duties towards children, in so far as it has duties towards anyone; in so far as anyone has duties towards anyone.

But when I was coming home from my music lessons in the evenings, before I knew it I had started walking along a particular street and gazing at a particular house, up at a particular window where sometimes there was a particular light and sometimes a particular darkness. I paused, but after a moment I was no longer safe from the imagined eyes which peered at me from countless windows, and I took to my heels and did not come to my senses until I heard my own heartbeats at the other end of the street. It is unbelievable how many souls a female creature can have, especially at night.

Yes, I had slammed the door on him; but was that not just

because I had, at that time, not yet fully convinced myself that I was pregnant? And if I longed to be with him now, was it not simply because I was now quite sure? And wanted to hang on to him? Perhaps even haul him to the altar? To such depths must a woman's thoughts stoop, because the child owns its mother and wants to drink her, and she must needs get herself a slave and set up with him that milk bar which is called marriage and was once a sacrament, the only sacrament which holy men might spit on; otherwise she must go about for life a woman of misfortune, carrying a love-sorrow like some sort of stone child in her system, with a live child by her side, an accusation against gods and men and a provocation to society, which had tried all it could to get rid of it for her, both born and unborn, but without success. To be brief, I loved him; and had slammed the door on him because a woman has many souls; and for that reason I now had no one definite to take twins out for a walk in a pram for me.

No. I took the same turning into the street again. It may well be that a pregnant girl will marry just anyone for she, like Nature, does not care very much what name is entered as the child's father by the pastor; but it was him, him, him I loved, despite everything and despite everything. Yes, this particular man; reserved, intelligent, clean; who had a vocation he would not divulge; and who looked at one with that secretly warm glance, enveloping but not piercing, so that things were never dead around him however much he was silent, and a girl was aware of him and no one but him in a crowded room; and went upstairs with him in silence afterwards; and he took her into his bed without first trying to persuade her by reciting a whole newspaper article over her; just as if nothing could be more natural. And when I shut the door on him on New Year's Eve he stayed on with me; and he stayed on with me because I had not let him in. If he had tried to persuade me with arguments or soften me with pleas I would perhaps have let him in finally, but he would then not have stayed on with me as soon as he left next morning; his arguments would have done no more, at most, than convert my mind. And if I met him now I would not with so much as a half a word give him a hint that I was pregnant, and least of all suggest that he should marry me; instead, I would say to him: I love you, and that is why I ask nothing of you; or else: I love you, and that is why I do not want to marry you.

ANOTHER GIRL AT NIGHT

And then suddenly I see a woman sitting on some steps. She is holding her bleeding head and sobbing aloud in the quiet of the night. Her handbag lies open on the pavement as if it had been thrown down, her mirror, lipstick, handkerchief, powder compact and money strewn all around. There was singing going on inside the house. I walked over to this woman to find out what the matter was; and it turned out to be Cleopatra.

"You reincarnate Skarpheðinn Njálsson, you are not crying, are you?" I said.

"Yes," said Cleopatra.

"What has happened?" I asked.

"They beat me up and threw me out," said Cleopatra.

"Who did?" I asked.

"Who but Icelanders?" she said. "These damned Icelanders."

"What for?" I asked.

"They didn't want to pay," she said. "First they tricked me into the house with them. Then they refused to pay. I shall kill those damned Icelanders, *by golly.*"

"Yes, but after all they are our countrymen," I said.

"I don't give a damn," said Cleopatra. "They refuse to pay. They beat you up and throw you out. And they take snuff."

"I'll get a doctor for you, Patra dear," I said, "and make a complaint to the police; and take you home."

"No-no-no," she said. "Not a doctor, and no complaint to the police, and least of all take me home."

"Home to our organist's," I said.

"I have no home," she said, "and least of all with him, even though I have been an overnight guest with his mother for four years just because he is a holy man. It was all right while there were Yanks. But now there are only a few strays left and they all have something steady, so I have to start scratching around like when I was a girl, and going home once again with Icelanders who take snuff and beat you up and refuse to pay. These damned sandy wastes and fellows in fettle! Dear darling Americans, Jesus let them come with the atom bomb quick."

"God help you, Cleopatra," I said. "Skarpheðinn Njálsson would never have spoken like that, not even if the axe Battle-Troll had been buried deep in the middle of his head."

"If I haven't got leave to feel sorry for myself then go away," said Cleopatra.

She had been given a bloody nose and a black eye, and there was a slight smell of Black Death off her; but she was more or less sober – she had no doubt sobered up with the beating, and was now only slightly fuddled. I gathered her belongings into her handbag and gave her the handkerchief so that she could wipe off the blood, and it was soaking at once, and my own handkerchief became soaked with blood too. I started thinking a bit, and came to the conclusion that this girl's blood and tears were of the same chemical composition as that of other girls, and so I invited her home with me to stay the night. She invoked God and Jesus over and over again on my behalf and I don't know what else, for it is just people like her who are the greatest theologians you can find. She stood up and I stood up, and under the first street-lamp she took out her lipstick and mirror and painted her mouth; and this performance moved me like a magnificent moral achievement in the middle of the night in this wicked world, so that I was ashamed of what an insignificant person I was.

She regretted how improvident she had been in the Yank business not to get herself decent accommodation, that's how stupid one could be, one hoped that the war would last for ever, and they were always throwing parties in those splendid huts with 'Kosykorners' and fancy lights, that was the life, *gee, man*. She had started with a sham colonel between Hafnarfjörður and Reykjavík, and ended up with a real colonel, grey-haired, and with diabetes. She had been at a Yank party with the Prime Minister, for the Americans are liberal-minded people because they have the atom bomb and make no distinction between prime ministers and girls. The colonel gave her a red coat and white bootees and the hat which was so broad-brimmed that one had to tilt one's head to get through a doorway; and money like dirt of course, man. *Gosh*. He had promised to come and fetch her when his wife died, but now he himself was dead, he could not endure the peace, probably his wife had killed him because she was young. And then Cleopatra started crying again; she had suffered a sorrow which was in every respect chemically correct and, what's more, precisely as spiritual as other sorrows, painful and yet wonderful, and I was sorry for her, even in earnest.

"That's how one loses everything and everything and everything," she said, "and dies, and has to start living again when one is dead. Isn't it fantastic that I who have been loved by a colonel should be beaten up by a nation which takes snuff?"

She had reached the age when the chemical changes which take place in a woman's body begin to make her disappointed with life, dead weary of the night roamings of youth; the adventure of the unknown no longer attracted her, youth's faith in something new and unique had turned into everyday bread-slavery – she was, truth to tell, just about ready to abandon these damned men of hers wherever they came from, some from the north, some from the south. She wanted a settled life, a fixed place, just like any other woman of thirty five. And, as she said, for that she had to have a little den of her own, not just living for ever off holy people who called you Cleopatra and lucky if is isn't Skarpheðinn in the Burning: "For of course my name isn't Cleopatra and never has been, still less anything else; my name is Guðrún, known as Guðrún the Wilderness."

I asked if she wanted to get married, but she did not know what to make of such an unseemly suggestion: "The very idea!" she said. On the other hand she confided to me, when we were in bed with the light switched off, that her dream of the settled life was a little flat with a living room and bedroom, carved Renaissance furniture, a kitchen, and a bathroom with a shower, and then to fix herself up with three steadies: one a married businessman with a little money, approaching his silver wedding; a seaman who was only ashore every now and again; and an educated young man who was engaged to an upper-class girl.

We discussed this idea at some length until we grew sleepy, and soon we lapsed into silence, until she said in the darkness after a good while, when I thought she was asleep, "Well, should we not be saying our Lord's Prayer now?"

"Yes," I said. "Say it for both of us."

She recited the Lord's Prayer, and then we bade one another Good night and went to sleep.

18

GENTLEMAN BEHIND A HOUSE

Although up-to-date writers say that it has a bad effect on children to rock them, I had all at once begun to take notice if there were something in the paper about cradles, even if it were only a cradle for sale. And now it was reported that the Town Council had defeated a Communist proposal to build a Day Nursery. "Woman" wrote to the papers and said that it would increase immorality in the country if such projects were subsidised from the public purse; the proper nurseries were the homes of true Christians and others of decent morals. But, I asked, why should there be nurseries only for the children of true Christians and those of decent morals? Why should there not be nurseries for the children of non-true Christians with wicked morals, such as me?

"We live in a society of people who have only one wish dearer than to care for rich children, and that is to kill poor children," said the Communist. "A few generations ago the rich were so powerful, even though they were still lice-ridden, that about half of all the children born in Iceland died. If the masses had no solidarity, the children of the poor would still be dying; and if we did not continue to strengthen this solidarity the rich would still be persecuting the poor and their children with direct measures taken in the name of Jesus, with scourgings and drownings, just as before. The opposition to a Day Nursery for the children of penniless mothers reveals clearly their way of thinking; they only need the lice to be precisely the same as in the days of the Fornication Act."*

I asked his friend, the bakery girl, "What would you do if you had a baby?"

Her smile vanished suddenly and her eyes widened, and she glanced questioningly at her Communist.

"It's safe to tell her," he said.

A woman asked for rye bread, and a girl for a cream cake, and then the shop was empty.

"Come this way," said the girl, and opened the flap of the counter and invited me inside; she took me through a tiny dark box-room, combined storage room and washroom opening out into a yard. There was fierce rain from the east, and black storm clouds were overhead. Outside in the mud stood a pram with its hood up and a sack spread over the whole thing to protect it from the worst of the weather. The bakery girl lifted the sack aside and, smiling, peeped in under the hood.

The baby was wide awake, and stared up from the bedclothes with huge eyes. When he saw his mother he squealed and

*In 1564 the Danish Governor of Iceland proclaimed a law under which adultery was to be punished with the death penalty.

kicked and pulled with all his might at one of his thumbs.

"My little darling," said his mother, and looked at her boy, entranced for a moment in the middle of the day's work, with black storm clouds over the back yard.

"Look what intelligent eyes he's got," I said. "What a fine gentleman he must be."

"If they found out that I keep him here I would be sacked," she said.

In the front of the shop an impatient customer had started to pound the counter.

ALL THE DOCTRINES OF THE WORLD — AND A LITTLE MORE BESIDES

Doctor Búi Árland came home smiling, with water streaming down his face, took off his soaked overcoat and said, "Well, now there is good news."

I waited.

"I think I can say with certainty that I have at last managed to squeeze a few thousand krónur out of Parliament for your father and his church."

"Oh?" I said.

He looked at me in amazement.

"And you do not throw your arms around my neck?" he said.

"Why should I?"

"For joy," he said.

"I have learned that Luther was the coarsest man who ever lived," I said. "So I have dropped the faith."

"Well I'll be damned!" he said, and took off his coat and wiped the water from his face, took off his spectacles and dried the raindrops from them. "After thinking it over, can we still not believe in the man even though he sometimes said *rectum* and *bumbus* in abominable German instead of Latin when he was engaged in disputation over the Holy Spirit? Or mentioned the genitals of an ass in some mysterious connection with the

Pope? He was still enough of a peasant to take Christianity seriously in the middle of the Renaissance, when the whole of Europe had stopped doing so; and rescue the movement; apart from the fact that he was fond of singing, like so many German peasants, poor wretch."

"I didn't know you were a Lutheran," I said.

"No, I did not really know it myself either," he said, laughing. "Not exactly. I had thought that I stood nearest to the one man in Christendom who demonstrably believes in nothing at all, namely the Pope. Except that I have made it a rule for myself to support old Jesus in Parliament, mainly because I agree with our uncrucified Jew-dog Marx that the Cross is opium for the people."

"In other words you are a materialist," I said.

"Why, what a long time it is since I have heard that word – in that denotation," he said. "We political economists use words, you see, in a slightly different sense. But since you have asked me in all sincerity about my religious beliefs, I shall answer you in the style in which you ask. I believe that E equals mc squared."

"What sort of rigmarole is that?" I asked.

"It is Einstein's Theory," he said. "This says that mass times the velocity of light squared equals energy. But perhaps it is materialism to hold that matter as such does not exist."

"And yet you take the trouble to procure money to build a church up in the far valleys for practically no one," I said.

"When I discovered some years ago that your father believed in horses, I vowed to myself to do everything I could for him. You see, I once had a religious revelation, rather after the manner of the saints. In this revelation it was revealed to me that horses are the only living creatures which have a soul – with the exception of fish; and this is due, among other things, to the fact that horses have only one toe; one toe, the ultimate of perfection. Horses have a soul, just like the idols; or the paintings of some artists; or a beautiful vase."

How smoothly he talked of the loftiest matters, almost absently, with that amiable civilised smile which was never quite free from sleepiness and could moreover sometimes end in a yawn, as indeed it did now; and he took out a cigarette and lit it. And while I contemplated him, the earth vanished from under my feet and my feet from under myself, and I had to muster all my strength not lose touch with substantiality altogether. I braced myself and said, "I heard today that the rich were once again going to make famine and murder the fate of illegitimate children, and pass laws that their fathers should be flogged and their mothers drowned – if only they dared to in the face of the solidarity of the masses. Is that true?"

"Yes," he said, and smiled amiably. "'All For Virtue' is our slogan, my good girl. Our wives want to have legitimate children, at least on paper; and preferably no competition. It is an an attack on the wives' class to have Day Nurseries."

"I do so want to put a question to you," I said.

"I wish I knew the answers to everything you asked," he said.

I asked: "Is it possible to be a Capitalist if one sees a baby child in a rainstorm behind a house?"

"That is a difficult question," he said, and scratched himself behind the ear. "I do not think I am far enough advanced to be able to answer it; at least I would first need to go behind a house."

"Why do Parliament and the Town Council not want my children to have a nursery like your children? Are my children not chemically and physiologically as good as your children? Why can we not have a society which is just as expedient for my children at it is for your children?"

He came right over to me and put his hand on the nape of my neck under the hair and said, "What has happened to our mountain-owl?"

"Nothing," I said, and hung my head.

"Yes," he said. "You have started thinking in a tight little circle from which you cannot break out. What is troubling you and getting worse every day?"

"I'm going," I muttered into my bosom.

He asked where, and when.

"Away, at once," I whispered.

"Tonight?" he said. "In this weather?"

"You have cast your vote against me and I have no home," I said; and then I told him what had happened to me and turned away, and he stopped smiling and there was a silence. Finally he asked, "Are you fond of the man?"

And I replied, "No. Yes. I don't know."

He asked, "Is he fond of you?"

"I haven't asked him," I said.

"Do you want to marry one another?" he asked, but I could not answer such an absurdity except by shaking my head.

"Is he short of money?" he asked. "Can I do anything for you?"

I turned to face him again and looked at him and said, "I have now told you something I have not even told him, and more I cannot do."

"May I then not ask anything further?"

"I don't even know what kind of a man he is," I said, "so there is no point in asking. I am a girl, that is all there is to it. And you have cast your vote against me. If I did not have my old and penniless parents up north my child would be born a convicted outlaw, as it says in the sagas, not to be fed nor forwarded nor helped nor harboured."

He looked at me questioningly, almost timidly, as if he were seeing a danger he had long feared from afar suddenly loom close, and repeated in the form of a question, rather foolishly, the words I had just used – "Did I cast my vote against you?" And he had the nail of one thumb between his teeth.

But when I made to walk away he followed me and said, "Do not be anxious, you can get from me all the money you want, a house, a Day Nursery, everything."

"You cast your vote publicly against letting me and others like me be called people, but want to make me your beggar in secret . . ."

"Why in secret?" he interrupted. "Between you and me there is nothing done in secret."

"No, now I am going, to have my baby with my own money," I said. "Anything rather than accept money secretly from someone."

I had no sooner got to my room than he had followed me, he even opened my door without knocking. Previously his face had momentarily tightened a little; for a while he had perhaps been on the verge of defending his point of view against me in earnest, but now his face had relaxed and he was once again gentle and unassuming, with that expression of candour that sometimes made him look more childlike even than his children.

"If I know our Red friends aright," he said, "it will not be long before they bring this matter up again. Perhaps it will be dealt with differently next time. I shall talk to my brother-in-law and other strong men in our party. There shall be a Day Nursery, good heavens, never fear."

"But if your brother-in-law says no?" I asked. "And the wives' class?"

"You are making fun of me now," he said. "Go ahead. The only consolation is – I do not consider myself much of a hero. But I promise you that in this matter I shall behave as if I were inspired by a woman . . ."

"A pregnant housemaid," I corrected him.

"A woman whom I have admired from the very first moment," he said.

"Yes, I once heard a tipsy man say that I was one of those women whom men want to go to bed with, without a word, the minute they see her for the first time."

He came over to me and embraced me and looked at me.

"There are one or two women so made," he said, "that a man forgets all his former life like a meaningless trifle the moment he first sets eyes on her, and is ready to sever all the obligations which tie him to his environment, turn around, and follow this woman to the end of the world."

"No, I shall not kiss you," I said, "unless you promise me never to give me money, but to let me work for myself like a free individual even though I am acquainted with you."

He kissed me and said something.

"I know that I am terribly stupid," I said afterwards. "But what am I to do? You are not like anyone else."

19

CHURCH-BUILDERS

Out of sight in a hollow to the east of the farm knoll rose the church; with a grassy slope behind the chancel. They had begun pouring the concrete the previous autumn, but had not had the money to buy a roof. The walls had stood in their moulds until now, springtime, when the money started to arrive from the Treasury to buy a roof. I was sitting down in the gulley beside the stream, where the smell of the reeds is stronger in winter than in summer; it was here that we had played as children with sheep's horns and jawbones, and filled a rusty tin can in the stream with the sort of water which could just as easily be cocoa, or mutton broth, or schnapps. And later there stood a tent here on the bank for three late-summer nights. And as I sat there I could hear above the murmur of the water the hammering of the church-builders alternating with the cries of the golden plover.

A long time ago there had been a church parish here of twelve farms, some say eighteen, but during the last century the church had been abandoned. Now another church was rising here, even though there were only three farms left in the valley – and the third farmer, Jón of Barð, the head carpenter, only counted as half or scarcely that, having lost his wife and with his children away in the south and fire no longer kindled in the farm except for the fire which burned within the man himself; and his faith the sort of horseman's faith which it would be more accurate to connect with the phallus than with Christ. Barð-Jón never called a church anything but "God's window-horse", nor the pastor anything but "the stallion of the soul-stud"; and neither I nor others were ever aware that he knew any other prayer than the old Skagafjörður Lord's Prayer which starts like this: "Our Father, oh, is that blasted piebald foal not tearing around all over the place again . . ." And that prayer he would mumble to himself all day long.

And Geiri of Miðhús laughed – that laugh which would suffice to build a cathedral, even on the summit of Mount Hekla. This many-childrened man, our neighbour, the other main farmer in the valley, was the incarnation of the most potent point of view in the world, the point of view which no argument can affect, neither religion nor philosophy nor economics, not even the arguments of the stomach, which are nevertheless always more sensible than the arguments of the brain, not least if it is the stomach of our children which is talking: this man said that he would never depart from this valley alive, accepted his pauper's grant, and laughed. He said that he hoped to God that if he had to bury any more unbaptised children it should be done at the church where Iceland's greatest man of renown had been baptised. He said that he himself was looking forward to lying for all eternity in one of those pleasant dry graves here in the uplands and rising from it when the time came in the company of the poets and heroes of old, rather than in a damp and tedious grave farther down in the district among the farm louts of today and slaves who fished the seas.

For most of the day they would discuss the saga heroes over their carpentry.

Barð-Jón was a particular devotee of those heroes who had lived on moors or on outlying skerries. He did not admire above all else the hero's poetry, but rather how long the hero could hold out alone against many in battle, quite irrespective of his cause; it made no difference to Geiri whether the hero was in the right or in the wrong. As a rule, heroes were in the wrong to begin with, he would say; they became heroes not through any nobility of cause, but simply by never giving up, not even though they were being cut to pieces alive. Of those heroes who had lived in the wilderness as outlaws he loved Grettir the Strong best of all, and for the same reasons as are enumerated at the end of *Grettir's Saga:* that he lived longer in the wilderness than any other man; that he was better fitted than all other men to fight with ghosts; and that he was avenged farther away from Iceland than any other hero, and what's more, in the greatest city in the world, away out in Constantinople.

My father's heroes were cast in a more human mould; they had at least to be lineal progenitors before they could engage his full confidence, and in particular they had to be poets. Mountains and outlying skerries were not the right setting for his heroes. This man of integrity, who had never taken a wrongful eyrir's worth from anyone, never found it remarkable that these heroes should have sailed with gaping dragon-heads and open jaws to Scotland, England or Estonia to slaughter innocent people there and plunder them of their possessions. Nor did this courteous upland farmer think it a blemish in the hero's conduct that he squirted his vomit into people's faces, bit people in the throat or gouged their eyes out with his finger as he walked past instead of raising his hat; and a saga woman could be none the less noble for having a destitute boy's tongue cut out for eating off her dish. I do not think there was a single incident in the *Saga of Egill Skallagrímsson* which was not more absorbing, nor indeed better known, to my father than all the important events which had taken place in the country during his own lifetime, and scarcely a couplet ascribed to Egill which could not come dancing off his tongue.

"My hero is, and always will be Þorgeirr Hávarsson," said Geiri of Miðhús. "And why? It is because he had the smallest heart in all the sagas put together. When they cut out that heart of his which had never known fear, not even in Greenland, it was no larger than the gizzard of a sparrow" –

and with that he laughed one of those laughs which would suffice to raise a cathedral.

The pastor thought nothing of calling in from farther down in the district, a five-hour ride, to take snuff and drive in a few nails with these entertaining believers. And now when the moulds were removed from the concrete walls it was seen that by far the largest window was on the east side, over the altar, looking out on to the slope where the meadow began to climb the hillside.

The pastor's expression was solemn that day, until at last he declared over coffee: "A tremendous revolution has taken place here – one of the greatest which has ever occurred in the history of mankind; and like all great revolutions it has happened silently, without anyone noticing it."

We had no idea where this was leading to, and waited.

"I do not know precisely how many churches have been built in the world since the introduction of Christianity," said the pastor. "But this is the first time in the history of mankind that any man has dared to design a church with a window over the altar. Previously, any church-builder who dared to do that would have been boiled alive."

Geiri of Miðhús brightened up and roared with laughter, for he thought the pastor was making yet another of his jokes.

Barð-Jón said, "It would not have been much of a window-horse if there had only been blank wall there."

"How lovely the hillside is," said my father.*

"How lovely the hillside is," echoed the pastor. "There, you see, the paganism in the sagas suddenly breaks through. The purpose of Christianity is that men should not see the hillside; and the purpose of a church is to shutter Nature from man's eyes, at least during divine service. In old churches, all windows were painted. And above the altar in every church in the world,

---

*The famous words spoken by Gunnar of Hlíðarendi, in *Njáll's Saga*, when he decided not to go into exile but to remain at home and brave his enemies instead.

even in our Lutheran churches, in all except this one, there hangs a picture or a symbol which leads man's thoughts towards the mysteries of holy faith and away from the delusions of Creation."

"Why then are you having a church?" I asked them. "What do you believe in?"

At that the pastor rose and came over to me and patted me on the cheek and said, "That's just the thing, my dear: we believe in the land which God has given us; in the district where our people have lived for a thousand years; we believe in the function of country districts in the national life of Iceland; we believe in the green hillside where Life lives."

THE GOD

Often I felt that these men were play-acting: the unreality of their role was their security – even their own destinies were to them saga and folk-tale rather than a private matter; these were men under a spell, men who had been turned into birds or, even more likely, into some strange beast, and who bore their magic shapes with the same unflurried equanimity, magnanimity and dignity which we children had marvelled at in the beasts of fairy tale. Did they not suspect, moreover, with the wordless apprehension of animals, that if their magic shapes were to be stripped from them the fairy tale would be at an end and their security gone, too, while real life would begin with all its problems, perhaps in some town where there was neither Nature nor mirage, no link with folk-tale and the past, no ancient path to the far side of the mountains and down to the river gulleys and out beyond the grass plains, no landmarks from the sagas? – only a restless search for sterile, deadening enjoyment.

"How can it occur to you, Father," I said, when the pastor and the church-builders had gone, "that it is possible to live off forty-five lambs when you know that a lamb only provides one single day's wage for a labourer? When you have received these forty-five days' wages for your efforts there are still three hundred and twenty days of the year left."

"We live," he said. "We live."

"And only two milk-meagre cows, dry in turns for half the year? And it says here in the paper that in America it is only considered an average day's work to make a hundred horse-loads of hay and look after a hundred and twenty cows and milk them."

"It also says in the paper there that in America forty million people would be blown to shreds on the first day of a nuclear war. All their milk would not help them then. So it is better to be an Eystridalur man in a dry grave and rise from it again in one piece beside one's church."

"Do you all then farm solely to be able to lie in a dry grave?" I asked

"I know perfectly well that it is impossible, according to arithmetic and scholarly books, to live in a far valley off a handful of ewes and two low-yield cows. But we live, I say. You children all lived; your sisters now have sturdy children in far-off districts. And what you are now carrying under your heart will also live and be welcome, little one, despite all the arithmetic and scholarly books. Here, moreover, life will be lived off one cow, and the child will thrive on it, long after Paris, London and Rome have become insignificant moss-grown heaps of rubble."

"But apart from the nuclear bomb, father," I said, "I still feel that you would be better to own even one stallion fewer and build yourself a privy instead."

"I know they have these privies in the south," he said. "But we have nature. If one considers human life from that particular standpoint, then nature is the best privy. And the horses, little one, they live in the mountains."

"I heard it said in the south that you actually believed in wild horses, father," I said.

"They say the most unlikely things sometimes, our friends in the towns," he said. "But it is quite true, on the other hand, that here in these parts it has long been the custom to reckon a man's worth in horses. No one ever thought much of a man in these parts who did not have a choice of horses if he had a journey to make. It's a fine sight in summer, the herd of brood mares; and a splendid beast, the stallion."

"It's even harder to understand that men who can use nature for their privy and who worship horses should build a church before anything else," I said.

"Man is that animal species which rides a horse and has a god," said my father.

"And builds a roof over God and lets the horses go roofless," I added.

"The herd looks after itself," said my father. "But the god is a domestic animal," he said, giving the word a neuter inflection.

"*The* God?" I said.

"*The* god," said my father. "Snorri Sturluson* inflected 'god' as a neuter, and I am not going to pretend to know better than he."

"What god is that, if I may ask?" I said. "To explain god would be to have no god, my little one," said my father.

"It can hardly be a Lutheran god," I said.

"Icelanders have always been taught that Lutheranism was forced on us by a German robber, King Kristian III of Denmark," said my father. "His Danish stewards beheaded Bishop Jón Arason.† We who work our farms up in the valleys of Iceland do not much care what gods are thought up by Germans and preached with murder by Danes."

"Perhaps then it was the late Papal god," I said.

"Rather Jón Arason than German Luther and those Danish kings," said my father. "But still that is not it."

*The great Icelandic historian, poet and saga-writer of the thirteenth century. He wrote *Heimskringla* (a history of the kings of Norway) and *Snorri's Edda*, a textbook of poetry and mythology.
†The last Catholic bishop of Hólar, one of the two sees in Iceland. He and his two sons fought bitterly against the Reformation and Danish oppression, and were executed in 1550.

I asked if he did not then want to change the church into a temple dedicated to Þórr, Óðinn and Freyr.

My father repeated their names slowly and thoughtfully, and his face softened again as if at the memory of departed friends: "Þórr, Óðinn and Freyr. Be blessed for naming them. But still it is not they."

"I think you do not know yourself what you believe in, Father," I said.

"Oh yes, little girl, I believe in my god, we believe in our god," replied this unfanatical believer, and smiled at our innocent chatter. "It is certainly neither a Lutheran god nor Papal god; still less a Jesus god, although that happens to be the one most often named in the pastor's prescribed reading; neither is it Þórr, Óðinn, Freyr, nor even the stallion himself, as they think in the south. Our god is that which is left when all gods have been listed and marked. No, not him, not him."

20

THE COUNTRY SOLD

The hammering faded into its own echoes and melted into the quiet of the mountain valleys; and still the plover was heard. Why not live for ever in tranquillity and peace, and fetch water from the stream instead of making it gush from an indoor tap? And no mixing machine? And the question of a privy still undecided?

Unfortunately, peace and tranquillity are only a poem to be recited in cities, the poem of country folk who have straggled into the towns through lack of money and there been infected by the great world bacterium; and soon not even a contemporary poem any longer, but a poem by Jónas Hallgrímsson. Would it strike any chord in a modern poet to hear a church being hammered together in a far valley and the golden plover calling in between the hammer blows? And the south-east breeze, which does not in fact exist in the south – where is the poet now who knows it?

Until the calm was suddenly shattered: the politicians had started screeching, there was to be an election. This unpleasant crew, which it was impossible to get rid of by any known device (the only consolation being to know of it at a distance), had now migrated to us for a while. Their words of abuse and mutual insinuations of crimes filled this tranquil, discreet-tongued valley. And the story repeated itself: even though country people heard them outlaw one another all day, and always with irrefutable evidence, it never occured to them to believe any of this mutual smearing, any more than it occurred to them to believe what the pastor said in the pulpit. When the candidates had concluded their addresses, the country people greeted them smilingly just as if they were ordinary plain folk.

A man who slaughters the wrong ewe in a district is excluded from the genealogies after his death, and his descendants, moreover, are branded for two hundred years; so it is little wonder that country people are sceptical of the misdeeds that the politicians prove against one another; indeed, they listen to the crime stories of political meetings in the same frame of mind as to saga-tales of throat-biting, vomit-squirting and the gouging out of eyes. And inasmuch as they are themselves guilt-less, whether because they have never had the opportunity to commit crimes or because they are holy men by nature, they find it as easy to forgive crimes as they find it difficult to believe them.

No power could have forced my father to believe, even had it been proved with hard facts before his very eyes, that there existed in Iceland people who wanted to hand over her sover-eignty to foreigners the year after the establishing of the Republic or, as it is called in modern terms, 'sell the country'. Right enough, it had happened once before in the sagas: Gissur Þorvaldsson and his associates had handed over Iceland's sovereignty to foreigners – sold the country. That crime, which the people of the valleys would have refused to believe in the year 1262,* they had now, after a seven hundred-year-long struggle for independence, forgiven with an historical forgiveness. If now there arose new politicians to sell their country, they would not believe it even though they saw it, but would forgive the crime with an historical forgiveness again when their descendants had struggled for another seven hundred years.

The politicians swore solemn oaths in the north that summer, no less than they had done in the south that winter: Iceland shall not be sold nor the nation betrayed, no atom station shall be built where Icelanders can be wiped out in a single day; at the very most a resting place will be allowed, out on Reykjanes in the south for foreign welfare missions. They swore it on the country, on the nation and on history, swore it on all the gods and sacred relics they claimed to believe in; swore it on their mothers; but first and foremost they swore it on their honour. And then I knew that now it had been done.

There was one further thing which gave me an indication: they had started the bones rigmarole again. They made fervent speeches about the Nation's Darling and called him our fellow parishioner, the freedom of the Icelandic nation had been his life, nothing would be left undone to find his grave and raise his bones from foreign soil and give them a stone because they had not been given bread while they were alive.

THE MAN THEY DID NOT UNDERSTAND
AND OUR MEMBER

The church-builders thought that the ones they supported,

*In that year, after a long period of power-seeking and civil strife, Iceland entered into a union with Norway, under the Norwegian crown.

and their opponents too, had all spoken well, just as much when they denounced one another's crimes as when they flocked together and swore oaths. Of course politicians, like everything else in their eyes, were just a type of saga, varyingly stout-hearted sea-raiders and clever brigands, who fought for other people's possessions with terms of abuse and false accusations instead of sword and spear; a modern saga, much duller of course than *Egill's Saga* or *Njáll's Saga*, but one which had to be read with the same kind of objective attitude. They recognised all the candidates, understood them all and forgave them all – all except the Communist. They could not understand a man who claimed to be the spokesman of the poor, and they felt it downright treachery against themselves even to say that poor people existed. They knew not only *Egill's Saga* and *Njáll's Saga* but also the Legendary Sagas. They were descended not only from the heroes of the sagas but from the prehistoric kings too. They were themselves vikings in disguise with invisible swords, even helmsmen of splendid ships. They got worked up whenever they referred to the Communist. They would much prefer to have forbidden such a man the right of speech. Did they, then, suspect him of wanting to make alliance with the wolf Fenrir* fettered in their own selves, which threatened to tear off the false saga-beards glued to their cheeks, strip them of the invisible sword of the champion and ditto the ship of the viking who ran breathlessly up the hillsides after a ewe and had never even set eyes on the sea?

"Did our Member . . . swear?" I asked.

"It was easy to understand what he was getting at, even though he did not put much in his mouth, the blessed old worthy," they replied, and from their answer I suddenly saw the mask he wore for his tired, penniless voters in the valleys of the north: an old worthy, something like an old and impo-

---

*In Scandinavian mythology, one of the monsters of darkness. He was fettered by the gods until, at the *Ragnarök* (destruction of the gods) he burst free and killed Óðinn.

tent bishop. But such men indeed would never have understood that he was himself too wearied of the sunshine of good days to have any ideals, too cultured to be affected by any accusations; that he looked on life as an empty farce or, much more likely, an accident; and was bored.

"By the way, he came over to me and asked me to greet the Good Stepmother," said my father. "And mentioned, moreover, that he would pay a visit up the valley to have a look at our church before he returned south."

I am not going to describe the mist which descended on me, or how the strength drained from my limbs; I was beside myself all day, and did I not dream all night that he was standing outside with the wooden ladle, ladling water out of the well? What well? There is no well there. Next day I heard nothing but hammer-blows and no plover; until I said to my mother, "If he comes, I shall run up into the mountains."

"And what do you want up in the mountains, my dear?" asked my mother.

"He shall never see me with a belly," I said.

Then my mother answered, "You do not have such a father that you cannot hold up your head before any man, whatever condition you are in; and, I hope, not such a mother either."

I am not going to describe how relieved I was when news came that he had flown south, without warning, on urgent business. But the next day brought a visitor to our door from down in the district, who had with him a letter for me, and on it the words: To Ugla.

His visiting card, with no signature, but with a new telephone number – that was all the letter; and these words hastily scribbled in pencil: "When you come, come to me; all that you ask for, you shall have."

21

ALL THAT YOU ASK FOR

All that you ask for, you shall have: little Guðrún was born in the middle of August or, by the way my father reckoned time, in the seventeenth week of summer. My mother said that the girl weighed 10 pounds. I was scarcely aware of the birth until she had been delivered; perhaps I am one of those who can have 10-pound babies ten times over without feeling it much. When my mother showed her to me I felt I did not know her, but I felt a little fond of her at once because she was so little and large. And my father, who never laughs, laughed when he saw her.

The church was completed at about the same time. While I was still confined they brought the altar from the old church out of the storage attic where it had been kept since the nineteenth century. Throughout my childhood that altar had stood in there among old lumber, and although it had become so faded that one could only just make out traces of an occasional saint and half a word of Latin here and there, I had always as a child been afraid of this relic which had some mysterious link with the Pope. When I was on my feet again the altar had been placed under that unorthodox gable-window in the church, and they had painted it red so that neither saint nor Latin could be glimpsed any more.

The other possessions of the church were a three-pronged and thrice broken brass candlestick, which I tied up with twine for them so that it would stay in one piece so long as no one touched it; and a copper candle-snuffer. With these oddments we were going to start so-called spiritual life anew here in the valleys of the north.

The pastor wanted to baptise little Guðrún at the same time

as the church was being consecrated; but when I told him that I had become scared of sorcery and exorcisms, and asked him if he did not feel it a grave responsibility to dedicate an innocent child to an institution which had been the arch enemy of human nature for two thousand years and self-confessed opponent of Creation, and asked if it would not be more prudent to keep the distance between gods and people as great as possible, he merely smiled and patted me on the cheek and then whispered to me in confidence: "Pay no attention to what I may recite from the manual with my lips; in our minds we shall dedicate her to the Hillside of Life."

The Women's Institute brought a Danish butter-god rising from a cream trough, but when the time came there was no place to hang it in the church and so they took the plaque away again. But they brought other things with them which were much more useful for the dedication of a church, no more nor less than a complete refreshment tent and all that went with it – coffee and chicory, and biscuits in the enormous quantities you can only see in the country, made from flour, margarine, granulated sugar and vanilla essence, in addition to layer-cake by the chestful. And though such baking might have been a touch anaemic, it played its part in saving the day's morale, for outside there was rain and a great deal of Black Death. And no one could expect dalespeople to provide coffee and all the trimmings for many districts, even though they happen to have knocked up a hut for God.

The pastor and the bishop made their two speeches apiece, and those who were sober crossed and uncrossed their legs and wriggled their toes and counted up to a thousand and from a thousand back down to one, over and over again all day long, until the speeches came to an end and the church was consecrated. Thereafter the pastor dedicated little Guðrún to the Hillside of Life, according to our agreement. At the end of the service the cement-spattered plank benches in the church were moved out into the tent, and later used for firewood. And after that the church stood empty, filled only with a smell of cement, with damp walls and the saints and the Latin painted over. When the temporary door had been put back into place (it had been made out of packing cases to last the next hundred years), it came to light that on the door were the following words, upside down, in black printed letters: Sunna Margarine Company. Finally a bar was nailed across the church door on the outside, for the State grant had not sufficed to provide a lock. Somehow it was as if everyone had a feeling that God would not be worshipped in this place again in the near future.

THE NORTHERN TRADING COMPANY

It rained very hard that evening. Near midnight we were relieved of the last drenched consecration guests, some of them being taken away by their friends, slung across their saddle bows. It had now been dark for some time. I was at the farm door with a candle, hanging up some rags to dry; the rain drummed on the slabbed paving, and through the open door came the warm fermented smell of hay, inseparable from the first shortening evenings. I had been hearing the dog barking busily for some time, but thought it was just the revellers being carried homewards down the valley; until all at once a man was standing in the doorway. First I heard his footsteps outside on the paving, then I felt him come nearer and gradually fill the doorway until all of him was there.

"Who's there?" I said.

He took a torch out of his pocket, much stronger than my candle, and shone it on me.

"Good evening," he said.

I thought I was going to turn to stone where I stood, but then replied questioningly and angrily in the way one would address a burglar: "Good evening?"

"It's me," he said.

"And so what?" I said.

"Nothing."

"What a fright you gave me, man."

"Sorry."

"It's past midnight."

"Yes," he said, "I didn't want to come during the daytime. I knew there were crowds of people here. But I wanted to see my daughter."

"Come right in out of the doorway, man," I said, and offered him my hand.

He made no attempt to kiss me or anything like that; caressing or coaxing was not in his nature. It was impossible to have anything but confidence in a man of his demeanour.

"Take off your things," I said, "you're soaking wet. How did you come?"

"The Cadillac's at the other side of the gulley," he said.

"The Cadillac!" I said. "Are you a thief now too?"

"The vocation," he said.

I told him he ought to explain this vocation, but he said it was impossible to explain a vocation.

"Have you left the police?" I asked; and he replied, "A long time ago."

"And now?" I asked.

"Plenty of money," he said.

"Plenty," I echoed. "If there is plenty, then it has quite certainly not been well come by. But come into the parlour anyway, or come into the kitchen instead, perhaps we'll see if there's any life left in the range. If not I'll try to get a fire going; you'll have to have some coffee even though I'm not sure if you'll be allowed to stay the night."

The kitchen was directly opposite the main door, with the parlour to the left and the living room to the right, where my parents slept.

"Where's my daughter?" he asked.

The outcome was that I took him into the parlour and shone the candle on the girl sleeping beside the wall, in the spare bed, with my place just in front of her. He looked at her, and

I at this unknown man, and found myself still in sympathy with those races which recognise no connection between father and child. For the moment I could in no way see nor understand that he could own this child any more than other men did, nor indeed that any man owns children generally. He stared at her for a long time without saying a word. I lifted up the bedclothes so that he could see all of her.

"Can you feel what a nice smell she has?" I asked.

"Smell?" he said.

"Children exude fragrance," I said, "like flowers."

"I thought they smelled of urine," he said.

"That's because you're a pig," I said.

He looked at me and asked solemnly, "Am I not her father?"

"Unless you want to deny it on oath," I said, and added: "Although I don't really see how it matters."

"It doesn't matter?"

"We won't go into that now," I said. "Come into the kitchen. I'll try to cheer the fire up a bit."

When he had sat down I noticed that his clothes were made of expensive material and his hat was new; and that his footwear was ill-suited for walking: his thin brown shoes had got covered in mud on the way over from the car, and he had waded through the stream. But when I offered him dry things he flatly refused them. "Not even well-knitted homespun socks?" I said.

"No," he said.

As usual, he had to be fed with conversational topics, he was reluctant to speak without prompting; but long after he had fallen silent the timbre of his voice would still tingle in one's ears.

"What news is there from the south?" I asked.

"None," he said.

"How is . . . our . . . organist?" I asked, and at the same moment was aware of the surrender implied in admitting our joint ownership of anything. And he was not slow to notice it either.

"*Our* organist," he repeated. "His mother is dead. But he is growing seven new kinds of roses."

I remarked how good it was to forget first and then die later, like that woman; and then I said that the world could not be utterly wicked, fundamentally, when there were so many varieties of roses in existence.

"And here's some layer-cake," I added. "We inherited it from the Women's Institute. Or would you rather have bread and butter with your coffee?"

Naturally he preferred bread and butter.

I could feel how he was watching me, even though I had my back turned to him as I busied myself with the food and coffee.

"And the gods?" I said, still rummaging through the corner cupboard.

"They have declared war on Pliers," said my visitor. "They claim that he had given them a half share in the Cadillac while he still believed in them, and allege that they have it in writing. So Pliers got rid of the car cheap."

"And you think it charitable to take the car off the poor creatures?" I said. "It was their pride and joy, after all, and I say for myself that I find it hard to imagine an atom poet without a Cadillac."

"I don't pity the gods," he said. "Vengeance is mine, saith the Lord."

"And how is the Figures-Faking-Federation getting on at selling the country?" I asked.

"Very well," he replied. "Pliers has flown to Denmark to buy the bones. The F.F.F. is going to hold a monstrous tile-hat funeral – for the people."

We carried on talking about this and that for a while, until suddenly, while I was laying the table, he said, staring at my hands, "May I be with you tonight?"

"Leave me alone, I'm a reinstated virgin," I said.

"What does that mean?" he asked.

"It's a girl who becomes a virgin again after seven years if she is left alone," I said, and hurried to the corner cupboard again so as not to let him see how I was blushing; it is really an act of sex to talk like that.

"We'll get married this autumn," he said.

"Are you mad, man? How can you get such nonsense into your head?"

He said: "It is expedient for us both; all of us; everyone."

"Wouldn't it be better for me to try to become a person first?" I said.

"I don't understand," he said.

"Can't you understand that I'm nothing, man?" I said. "I know nothing, can do nothing, am nothing."

"You are the ultimate thing in a northern valley," he said.

"I think it enough to have a baby with the first one who offered, without making things worse by marrying him."

"Why did you slam the door on me last year?" he asked.

"Why do you think?"

"Another man, maybe," he said. "And myself fallen out of favour."

"Of course," I said. "Always another and another, a new one and another new one. I could scarcely cope with the numbers I slept with."

"Why are you behaving like this?" he said.

"Tell me more of the south," I said. "Tell me at least what you have become. I don't even know whom I'm talking to."

"Tell me what you want to become," he said.

"I want to learn children's nursing," I said, and thereby made him the first to hear what I had long been thinking to myself.

"Nursing other people's children?" he asked.

"All children belong to society," I said. "But obviously society will have to be changed in order to make it treat its children better."

"Change society!" he said contemptuously. "I've become tired of such talk."

"You've also become a criminal, just as I thought."

He said, "When I was at home, as a boy, I discovered

Communism on my own, without reading about it in books. Perhaps all poor boys in the country and towns do it, if they are right in the head and are fond of music. Then I went to school and forgot Communism. Finally I got my vocation and unhitched the hack, as I told you last year. Now comes the test of whether I am a man in the society in which I live."

"We live in a criminal society, and everyone knows it; those who gain by it know it, just as well as those who lose by it," I said.

"I don't care in the least," he said. "I only live once. I shall show them that an educated person who is fond of music does not need to become their lackey if he himself doesn't want to."

I contemplated him for a long time across the table as he ate and drank.

"Who are you?" I asked finally.

"The Cadillac's at the other side of the gulley," he said. "If you want to, drive away with me tonight."

"I could best believe that you are the Deacon of Myrká,"* I said.

He reached into his breast pocket and brought out a bulging wallet, opened it beside his coffee cup, and pulled out half of its contents, bunches of 100 krónur notes and 500 krónur notes like new packs of playing cards, fresh from a bank: "The Northern Trading Company," he said. "Cars, bulldozers, tractors, mixing machines, vacuum cleaners, floor-polishers: everything which whirls, everything which makes a noise; modern times. I'm on my way south from my first trading trip."

I reached out my hand for the notes and said, "I'll burn them for you, my lad."

---

*Folk-tale: a deacon from Myrká was drowned when riding to fetch his sweet-heart to a Christmas party. His ghost arrived to pick up the young woman, and tried to take her with him into his grave. She escaped with difficulty, "and was never the same again afterwards".

He pushed them back into his wallet and returned it to his pocket.

"I'm not above people, as the gods are, much less above gods, as the organist is," he said. "I am a person, money is the only reality. The reason I show you my wallet is so that you should not think me mad."

"Anyone who thinks that money is reality is mad," I said. "That's why the organist burned the money and then borrowed a króna off me for boiled sweets. And now I shall let you into a secret in return: there is another man who affects me even more powerfully than you, I have only to know of him 100 kilometres away for my knees to go weak. But do you know what makes me afraid of him? He has a thousand times more money than you; and he has offered to buy me anything in the world which money can buy. But I have no wish to become a million-krónur lie in female form. I am what I can be on my own earnings. I would perhaps have invited you to stay the night if you had come here penniless, yes, perhaps even have gone away with you tomorrow morning, on foot. But now I cannot invite you to stay the night; nor drive away with you, either."

22

SPIRITUAL VISITORS

One autumn night I woke up in the greyness which precedes dawn; and to the best of my knowledge it was our pastor outside on the paving talking to my father through the living room window. Soon I heard the footsteps of visitors at the farm door. I dressed in a flash and saw to the child, but while I was tidying up the spare room, where my daughter and I stayed, the visitors came in.

It seemed at first glance an ominous sight to see a pastor,

sober, and without warning, in a remote parish-of-ease at that
time of day, but the balance was restored by the fact that on
this occasion he had picked himself companions who well
befitted a true pastor on an unexpected journey – the gods
themselves. I am not going to describe the shock it gave me
to see the two rascals, those phenomena who had done most
to turn tarmac into folk-tale in my memories, crossing a
threshold north of the mountains in the flesh. But this was
clearly neither the time nor the place to indulge in stupid
witticisms: the Joint-Stock Company Earnest was deeply
imprinted on the expressions of the visitors – I am tempted
to say, the Murder Corporation Solemnity; the atom poet
Benjamin strode through the mountains with his face to the
skies, and in Brilliantine's eyes there lurked that unique
shallow stab of insanity which is practically made for
bewitching a pastor, yes, even for beguiling a girl in a garden
behind a house.

"Where are the twins?" I asked.

"I promised the wife to shoot them a lamb," said Brilliantine,
and bared those smooth glistening front teeth.

"Fancy you up here in the country," I said to the atom poet,
who had flopped exhausted on to our divan.

"The whole world – one station," he replied. "And I
Benjamin, this little brother."

"They do not come empty handed," said the pastor.

"We were sent," they said.

I asked by whom, but the pastor was quicker and said, "They
have a mission."

"We were sent by the godhead," they said.

"Which godhead?" I asked.

"These young men are instruments," said the pastor.
"Remarkable instruments. Hmm. In response to inspiration
they have brought with them here to the north the earthly
remains of the Darling. They have received a command of a
kind I do not care to call into question. And at the same time,
our dear district's age-old dream seems about to be fulfilled."

"Well, well, is that so?" said my father, and looked at the visitors with a benevolent smile. "And who are your people, boys?"

"We belong to the atom bomb," they said.

At this reply my father's face stiffened and his smile vanished as if he had heard something flippant and cheap.

The pastor said that the boys were rather sleepy.

"One is a poet and singer and former message boy with the joint-stock company Snorredda," I said, "and the other is a model family man and owner of twins, former storekeeper with the same enterprise: both friends of mine from the south."

"Great believers, and they have had a remarkable experience," said the pastor. "I do not call anything of that kind into question."

"We don't believe," corrected the god Brilliantine. "We are. We have direct contact. We could, moreover, have become millionaires long ago if we had so wished; perhaps got to Hollywood, what's more."

"We are at war," said Benjamin. "He who does not believe in us shall first be crushed, then wiped out. We shall not cease before we have stolen everything and broken everything. Then we shall burn everything. Down with Two Hundred Thousand Pliers! We shall not even spare Portuguese Sardines nor Danish Dirt. Am I mad or am I not mad?"

My father had gone out. The pastor nodded to himself over these remarkable instruments of the Almighty, and offered them a pinch of snuff, but they only wanted to puff their own cigarettes; on the other hand, the pastor was allowed to light them for them.

"This silence will drive me mad," said Benjamin.

"Isn't there a wireless?" asked Brilliantine.

After a short while they were both asleep, one on the divan and the other on the bed. I removed their cigarettes, from the mouth of the one and the fingers of the other, so that they would not set themselves on fire while they slept.

PORTUGUESE SARDINES AND D.L.

"A symbolic event of historic significance has taken place in the life of this nation," said the pastor. "Today this remote valley is once again the centre of national life, as it once was long ago in the day when the Nation's Darling was brought in swaddling clothes here to this Eystridalur church. The champion of Icelandic freedom and the poet of our spirit is once again home in his valley; our trinity – star of love, ptarmigan, and dandelion hillside – welcome anew that friend whom a blind nation lost in a foreign graveyard for a hundred years. But while he lay there hidden without a headstone, all his ideals were realised, and Iceland's every cause did triumph. The Icelandic people greet . . ."

There could be little doubt about it – our pastor had already composed his funeral speech, and was trying it out on me.

"But my dear Pastor Trausti," I said, when he had rattled on for a bit, "in our minds he has never died. That's why we have never made a fuss about his so-called bones nor his lack of a headstone in Denmark. He dwells in the blue mountain peaks we can always see when the weather is fine."

In the back of a big truck at the other side of the gulley were two crates, each of about the capacity of a barrel; and when it was broad daylight my father and I walked over with the pastor to examine these wares.

"Two crates," I said. "He hasn't half grown bulky from not existing for a hundred years."

"Yes, it is undeniably a little odd," said the pastor. "But they set off in a great hurry. They say that one of the crates is undoubtedly the right one."

We examined the crates and found addresses printed on them: "Prime Minister of Iceland" on the one, and "Snorredda Wholesale Company" on the other – two names for the same enterprise. Then my father noticed that on one crate the following words had been tarred in Danish – "*Dansk Ler*".

"What do these words mean?" he asked.

"*Dansk Ler, Dansk Ler,*" muttered the pastor pensively. "That is just like the Danes. That nation invariably tries to insult us Icelanders."

"It means, at its best, Danish Clay," I said. "Should we not first take a look into the other crate? It looks more promising to me even though I don't understand the foreign writing on it."

We prised up one of the planks of the lid with a crowbar, and I groped among the packing for the contents; and what did I pull out but a small tin, about 200 grams in weight, wrapped in semi-transparent paper? I recognised the merchandise quickly enough from my pantry work in the south: Portuguese Sardines imported from America, that fish which the papers said was the only fish which could scale the highest tariff walls in the world and yet be sold when ten years old at a thousand per cent profit in the greatest fish country in the world, where even the dogs walk out and vomit at the mere mention of salmon.

"Miracle fish, to be sure," I said, "but not quite the miracle we expected."

"We shall not open the other crate," the pastor said then. "We shall let faith prevail there. In actual fact it is irrelevant what the crates contain. This is a symbolic consignment. At a funeral it is not the chemical contents of the coffin which matter, but the memory of the deceased which lives on in people's hearts."

But by then my father had opened the second crate and taken the packing out through the opening. And it was just as I had suspected – in that crate too there was not much which was likely to enhance the nation's prestige. But yet, if one believes that man is dust and dirt, as the Christians believe, then this was a man the same as any other; but not an Icelandic man, for this was not Icelandic dirt; it was not the gravel nor earth, sand nor clay, which we know from our own country, but a dry, greyish calcareous devil like nothing else so much as old dog's dirt.

"Well," I said, "is the Nation's Darling Danish Clay or Portuguese Sardines?"

"Do you believe in nothing, little girl?" said the pastor.

"A prank!" said my father, and walked off to see to his horses.

"Do *you* believe?" I asked the pastor.

Suddenly there was a hard expression around the mouth of this cheerful kindly man who was normally the least orthodox of men, something adamant and dogmatic – I am inclined to say hard-hearted – so that I scarcely knew him for the same person; and there came a cold gleam of fanaticism into his eyes.

"I believe," he said.

"Do you believe in just the same way, when you can touch it and see clearly that it is the opposite of what you thought?" I asked.

"I believe," he said.

"Is it then belief to believe what one knows with absolute certainty is not so?" I asked.

"I believe," said Pastor Trausti, "in the function of country districts in the national life of Iceland. This clay, which perhaps preserves the sap from the bones of the freedom hero and great poet, is to me a sacred symbol. From now on it shall be an article of faith for Iceland that the Nation's Darling is once more back in his own valley. The Holy Spirit in my breast enlightens me in this Icelandic belief. I hope that our district will never again let go of this symbol of its faith in itself."

Then he looked out over the valley between the mountains and said in a solemn altar voice, with an exalted glow in his eyes: "May the Lord for ever bless this our district of districts."

THE HORSES

The silence woke the gods after a short while, and my mother brought them hot coffee. When they had inhaled a few more cigarettes they went out with a gun.

It was one of those tranquil autumn days which sometimes come to the valleys, when a tiny sound awakens echoes out of distant cliffs. It was not long before the mountains on both sides of the valleys reverberated with gunfire, and this peaceful valley beyond the world was stricken with panic: autumn birds dashed past in violent flight, sheep halfway up the mountain slopes formed into file and headed for the wilderness; and the snorting horses surged away up and down the mountain.

One of the loveliest and most magnificent events which can happen in the country is when horses take fright, particularly in a herd. A meadow pippit has flown past. The horses' fear is at first blended with play, even with mockery, amusement touched with a shudder, not unlike the behaviour of the mentally ill. They trot as if they were retreating from a slow-moving stream of fire, but with lightning in every action, storm in every nerve, swinging their heads everywhere as if the front of their necks were made of elastic, gracefully flirting their tails. They can even pause for a moment, and start biting and boxing, with those romantic mating cries of theirs. Then all at once it is as if the fire has started flowing right under these strange creatures, they charge away like a storm incarnate over scree and bogs and landslides, dipping the tips of their toes for a fractional moment into the furnace which blazes beneath their hooves, cutting across waterfalls, gullies and boulders, galloping steeply for a while until they stand trapped at last on some ledge high in the mountain-tops, there to die and be eaten by birds.

The gods returned just before noon. They had succeeded in shooting one lamb, and had dragged it between them down off the mountain; Brilliantine, this sole Luther of the present, as skilled a family man as he was an interpreter of religious mysteries with the help of the Spirit, did not venture to return home empty handed to his wife and twins.

My father groped for the lamb's ear and recognised the mark of one of the farmers in the district, and said that this would come before the sheriff unless they paid for it and excused it as an accident. They found it a harsh doctrine that one should not be allowed to shoot the sheep which ran wild in the mountains, and asked what farmers lived on if they could not shoot sheep.

A little later they toppled the crates off the truck and called on the pastor to come along. Nothing could shake Pastor Trausti's conviction that they were the instruments of Higher Powers, if not manifestations of the godhead itself as they themselves claimed; he said that he was a Lutheran pastor, and that he believed those who let themselves be governed directly by the Holy Spirit and understood holy writ without the mediation of the Pope. The pastor's last words to us as he climbed up into the truck with them were that within two days he would come back here to the valley with a congregation and some district worthies, and give the Nation's Darling a proper funeral.

After further consideration, the herd of horses had left off being frightened at all and had calmed down, and were now grazing in the home pastures, on the grass fields and gravel banks or in the home meadow close up to the farm. I stood at the window in that autumn light which makes the dead and the living more sharply discernible than the light of any other season. Yes, what a well-sculptured creature the horse is, so finely carved that even if there were no more than half a chisel stroke extra the workmanship would be ruined; that curve from neck to rump, and all the way down to the fetlock, is in actual fact a woman's curve; in the oblique-set eyes of these creatures lies buried a wisdom which is hidden from people but blended with the mockery of the idols; around the muzzle and the underlip hovers the smile which no movie star has ever been able to reproduce; and where is the female star who smells as wonderful as the nose of a horse? And what about the hoof, where all the world's fingers end: claw and cloven hoof, hand and flipper, paddle and paw, fin and wing. And probably because the horse is such perfection, the horse's token, the horseshoe, is our token of faith over all our doors, the symbol of good fortune in fertility and woman, the opposite of the sign of the Cross.

When the peace of autumn has become poetic instead of being taken for granted . . . the last day of the plover become a matter of personal regret . . . the horse become associated with the history of art and mythology . . . the evening ice-film on the farm stream become reminiscent of crystal . . . and the smoke from the chimney become a message to us from those who discovered fire – then the time has come to say goodbye. The world-bacterium has overcome you, the countryside has turned into literature, poetry and art; and you no longer belong there. After one winter in the company of electric floor polishers, farmer Falur's house in the valley has become only a brief shelter for the girl in the poem "Snow swirls across the hills"*, in order not to die of exposure. I had long begun to count the days until I could once again leave home, where I felt an alien, and go out into the alien world, where I was at home. But still I paused for a while over my thoughts of departure, and listened to the silence which had robbed the gods of sleep; and dusk sank slowly over the horses.

That same night, near bedtime, Government messengers arrived in police cars to fetch the Portuguese Sardines and D.L.

---

*By Jónas Hallgrímsson: it is about a mother who is caught with her child in a blizzard. The mother dies of exposure, but the child survives.

23

PHONING

"I'm sorry for phoning, and so late; but I've come. And you wrote that I should come to you . . . first; at once. I have been hoping that you know of some job or other. But now I'm not going to tell you how I feel about phoning like this; to be such a peasant as to take politeness seriously . . . not even changed out of my travelling clothes, and covered with dust from head to foot."

"Dust, who is not dust? I am dust. But I am your Member of Parliament . . . nevertheless."

"Yes, but do you know whether I vote for you?"

"I was asked to take a little parcel with me in the plane south this summer on behalf of a political opponent, a woman from the Ós district who has just gone south to have her gums cleaned out and had forgotten her eiderdown, and was lying in bed in the south with nothing to keep her warm in the middle of her toothlessness. I said of course, naturally . . ."

"Yes, I am just exactly like that woman . . ."

"Except that you have a full complement of teeth and choose me – perhaps, some time. In a word, I am your Member, whomever you vote for. Where are you?"

"In a public phone box; standing in the middle of the square with a wooden case."

"And with nowhere definite to stay the night, of course."

"Yes, perhaps – at my organist's."

"Are you with . . . the little one, what was her name again?"

"Her name is Guðrún, and she's staying in the north until I have managed to fix myself up."

"And what are your plans?"

"I want to become a person."

"What do you mean, a person?"

"Neither an unpaid bondwoman like the wives of the poor, nor a bought madam like the wives of the rich; much less a paid mistress; nor the prisoner of a child which society has disowned. A person amongst persons. I know it's laughable, contemptible, disgraceful and revolutionary that a woman should not wish to be some sort of slave or harlot; but that's the way I'm made."

"Don't you want to get a husband?"

"I don't want to get a slave, neither under one name nor another."

"But at least you want to get a new coat?"

"I neither want to make a poor man dress me in rags nor a rich man dress me in furs, for having slept with him. I want to buy myself a coat for money which I have earned for myself because I am a person."

"I can cheer you up with the news that from now on no one need become a Communist for lack of a Day Nursery. Indeed, the new authors say that only scoundrels rock their children, and only sadists sing "Hushabye Baby", so you must not think it was a painless matter getting Town Council agreement on such a perilous project. I shall not attempt to conceal it from you: we sweated profusely, and trembled considerably, even foamed at the mouth . . . a little; also, 'Woman' had published reams and reams in the papers saying what a scandal it was to have the children of Communists rocked at the public's expense. Finally, I betrayed my party over it, and another member did likewise for my sake; and, as I said, it scraped through."

"Well, it's time to say goodbye and thank you for everything."

"Is that all – when I have become a party renegade for your sake?"

"No, I thank you especially and particularly for your wanting me to phone; and then of course for everything else. And I beg pardon that I did as you asked. Even when you mean nothing with what you say, you can get me to do everything

I don't want to do. I know I'm a fool, but what am I to do? Well, now I'm going on my way, Good night. My greetings to everyone."

"Wait a moment, I'll drive through the square in three minutes . . ."

PATAGONIA

I think that was our conversation, as nearly as one can recall a conversation when a girl talks to a man and a man to a girl, for of course the words themselves say least of all, if in fact they say anything; what really informs us is the inflection of the voice (and no less so if it is restrained), the breathing, the heart-beat, the muscles around the mouth and eyes, the dilation and contraction of the pupils, the strength or the weakness in the knees, as well as the chain of mysterious reactions in the nerves and the secretions from hidden glands whose names one never knows even though one reads about them in books; all that is the essence of a conversation – the words are more or less incidental.

And when this conversation was over, I felt a marvellous elation in the blood and my heart was beating as if I were high on a mountain; I had lost all substance and everything was possible from now on, with every trace of weariness gone.

Three minutes, I thought; no, it's quite out of the question, I'll run. How could it ever occur to me, even though he had scribbled it lightheartedly on his card? To tell the absolute truth it had not really occurred to me at all; that whole day, on my way through unfamiliar country, I had in fact been thinking: what absolute nonsense, this was the very last thing which could ever have happened to me; I had not even allowed such foolishness to reach the surface of my thoughts; I had been looking at Nature out of the bus window, and had decided in my own mind where I was going to stay the night: some distant relatives in town would, out of affection for the north country, allow a girl from the north to stay the night. But how hot my cheeks had felt; and I had not been able to get any food down in three counties, except a caramel and some soda-water in Borgarfjörður. On the ferry from Akranes an extremely ugly woman had stared at me wherever I went, and I had the impression that she would walk over to me when least expected and say, "Of course you're going to phone him." I had wanted to hit this woman. It would be not merely rude-ness to phone him, but a breach which would never be healed, and above all a surrender, I almost say the ultimate surrender, that unconditional surrender which was talked about during the war and which no victory can ever follow, ever. The ferry had slid to the quayside – and what had happened to that ugly woman? She had gone. And I had stepped from the ferry on to land – and straight to this phone box on the square; and phoned. But as I said, now I was going to run.

He was standing beside me in the square; he said Hello and offered me his hand with that gentle nonchalant lightness of a man whom nothing can affect – in the first place because he has a million, and in the second place because everyone is to be hanged tomorrow; such was his unique, incomparable charm.

"Let's go," he said.

And before I knew it he had picked up my wooden case, that laughable receptacle made in a mountain valley where no one knew what a suitcase was – this man who flew between countries with a case made of soft fragrant yellow leather which creaked. He carried this trash of mine to his glossy burnished car which stood at the kerb a few paces away. And before I knew it I was myself sunk deep in the seat beside him; and with a touch, the car rolled soundlessly off into the traffic.

"Aren't you afraid," I asked, "of letting the town see such a country bumpkin getting into your car?"

"I am always getting braver," he said, changing into third. "Soon I shall be a hero."

We drove on in silence for a moment.

"Where are we going, anyway?" I asked.

"To a hotel," he said.

"I who gained nothing all summer except little Guðrún!" I said. "How do you expect me to have the money to sleep in a hotel? To tell the truth I don't know what I'm doing in your car. I must be mad."

"How's Guðrún?" he said.

"Thank you," I said. "She weighed 10 pounds."

"Congratulations," he said. "Incidentally" – and he glanced at me as we turned a corner: "I seem to recall that we were on less formal terms?"

"Will you please let me out now?" I said.

"In the middle of the road?" he said.

"Yes, please."

"Can I then not invite you to stay the night?"

"No thanks," I said.

"That's odd," he said. "I am always invited to stay the night whenever I come north."

He slowed the car, and I saw that we were in front of the business premises of the Snorredda company. He drove round a corner and through a gate, stopped, stepped out, opened the door for me and locked the car. And once more I was with a man behind a house at night, except that here there was no need to be afraid of anyone in the windows. He took me through a little back door, up some steep narrow back stairs laid with multicoloured rubber flooring so clean that no one seemed ever to have trodden on it before; and I followed him higher and higher, I don't know how high, perhaps up through the roof; it was like a dream – perhaps one of those dreams of uncertain joy which end in a feeling of suffocation and nightmare; or was it the beginning of my becoming a person? Finally he opened a door for me, and I stood in a little hall and could see through a half-open door into a room – leather-covered furniture, a desk in the middle of the floor, books on shelves, a telephone, a wireless.

"Where am I?" I asked.

"This is my hideout," he said. "There's a bathroom over there, a little kitchen here. Further in from the living room is the cubbyhole where I sleep, but tonight I shall lend you my bed and I myself shall sleep outside the door."

"But your home?" I asked.

"Where in the world is shelter sure?" he said, and smiled wryly at this hymn-opening.

"Why shouldn't there be?" I said.

"My wife is in California," he said.

"And Fruit-blood?"

"I sent her to a convent school in Switzerland."

"And Jóna's Day-beam?" I asked.

"That Småland-American female saviour had started to beat my little angel with a cudgel night and day for saying Hell. So I fired the old hag, boarded out the children and shut up the house. It has been empty ever since."

The bathroom was inlaid with pink tiles and the water from the hot springs was fragrant in the tub. One whole wall was a mirror from floor to ceiling, and I stared amazed at this big strong woman who stood there with milk in her breasts, and regretted having to put on my clothes again and become a penniless girl from the north once more, and I dawdled as much as I could. At last there was nothing left but to chew some soap, and then I went out into the living room.

He was sitting on a chair reading a book, and had fried some ham and eggs and laid the table; water for the tea simmered in a glass electric kettle beside him. He motioned to me to sit down in an armchair on the other side of the table and started to make the tea.

And I stared at this man in a trance, this fairy tale personified: the man who owned the world, not just all the wealth which one could reasonably wish for; the man who enjoyed all the power to be had in a little country – and what is the difference between a little country and a large one except in degree? – but quite certainly endowed with soul, no less than the horses which had once appeared to him in a divine vision; healthy, intelligent, handsome, virile, in the prime of life, his every word a poem, his every thought a joy, his every movement a game; in reality such a man is above everything on earth, a phenomenon in the sky – and how are the thoughts of an earth-bound pauper to be anything but a tasteless joke and dreary drivel in his eyes and ears?

"Is there anything more ludicrous than a penniless girl from the north who says she is going to become a person?" I said.

"All that you ask for, you shall have," he said.

I still did not have much of an appetite, but I drank the tea he had made and enjoyed it.

"By the way," I said, "where do these words come from?"

"I wrote them when I learned the truth," he replied.

"The truth?" I echoed.

"Yes, it's little wonder you laugh," he said. "You think I have become a theologian like Jóna and started hopping."

"It depends on which truth it is," I said.

"Quite so," he replied. "The religious hero says, 'Truth shall make you free'; and in that case truth is perhaps merely the fact that Jón Smyrill of Brauðhús* was born into the world – which is, in fact, a matter of dispute, historically; or that foul fellow Muhammad – which *is* indisputable, certainly. But that is not what I mean. Do you remember once, last year, I told you Einstein's Theory of Relativity? That is not what I mean, either, even though it is proved by calculations; nor even that simple, unforgettable and irrefutable truth of junior school, that water is H_2O."

I said I was becoming curious.

"I mean the truth of myself," he said, and looked at me without his spectacles. "The truth of my own nature. That is the truth I have discovered, and if I do not live that truth my life is but half; in other words, no life at all."

*An old Icelandic scholastic "translation" of *Jesus Christ of Nazareth*: *Jón* and *Jesus*, the two commonest names in both countries; *Smyrill*, the anointed one; *Brauðhús* (breadhouses), from the Hebrew etymology of *Nazareth*.

I asked, "Which is your truth?"

"You," he said, dropping into the intimate form of address. "You are my truth: my life's truth. That is why I offer you everything a man can offer a woman. That is what I meant when I wrote to you on that card."

I give you my sacred oath that I lost my sight completely and died.

"Don't you see these rags I am in from Sauðárkrókur?" was the first thing I said when I came to life again; also using the intimate address.

"No," he said.

"I know no languages except Zoëga's *English Primer*," I said.

"Really?" he said.

"And play the harmonium, which in itself is ridiculous even if one plays it well; and have never had varnish on my nails nor scarlet on my lips except at the most perhaps off some red fruit-soup; and you accustomed to women who look as if they had drunk black bull's blood and scratched raw human flesh."

"Yes, all that is precisely what I meant," he said. "That's why I am turning over a new leaf."

"But when you have slept with me for a night, or two nights, or even three at the very most, you will awake from your torpor and look at me, horrified, and ask just as in a folk-tale: Whence came this witch into my bed? – and then you will steal softly away from me before dawn and never come back again."

"What do you want me to do?" he said, "and I shall do it."

I gazed at him for as long as I could, then down at my knees; but I could make no reply.

"Do you want me to renounce everything?" he said. "The company, the constituency, public posts, party, acquaintances, friends? – and be once again a plain penniless man of culture?"

"I could never, never bear to have you lowered by a hair's breadth on my account," I said. "Besides, I am sure that though you were penniless you would carry on being what habit has made you, the man you are; and I what I am, a country bumpkin, a housemaid, common; nothing but a longing to become a person, to know something, to be able to do something for myself, not to have everything paid for me, to pay for myself. Where would a place exist for both of us?"

"Now you must see that Patagonia is not such a bad idea after all," he said.

"Does any Patagonia exist?"

"I shall show it to you now on the map."

"Isn't it some barbarian land?" I asked.

"Is it not all the same?" he replied. "Soon the whole world will be one vast barbarian land."

"And there was I, thinking that world civilisation was just beginning," I said. "I thought we were beginning to be people."

"The attempt seems to have failed miserably," he said. "No one any longer imagines for a moment that it is possible to save Capitalism, never mind resurrect it; not even with Poor Law Relief from America. Barbarianism is at the door."

"Is Communism barbarianism then?"

"That is not what I said," he replied. "On the other hand, Capitalism will drag world civilisation down with it to the depths when it falls."

"Iceland too?" I asked.

He said, "There exist land and sea, divided between east and west; and the atom bomb."

"Has Iceland then been abandoned to – the atomic war?" I asked.

Suddenly he rose to his feet, turned away and walked over to the wireless, and switched off some Spaniard who was making a speech on the other side of the world.

"The conflict is between two fundamentals," he said. "The battlefield covers all lands, all seas, all skies; and particularly our innermost consciousness. The whole world is one atom station."

"And Patagonia too, then?"

He had managed to find some light music somewhere on the instrument. He came over to me and sat down on the arm of my chair and put his hand on my shoulder.

"Patagonia is a different matter altogether," he said. "Patagonia is the land of the future in the middle of the present, the land which has always been what Europe and the United States have yet to become: a wasteland where a few ignorant shepherds look after sheep. I hope you understand that the world in which I have lived is doomed and that there can be no appeal against that sentence; and further, that I do not care, that I am losing nothing if I renounce it all. The decision is yours. Say what you want."

24

THE SQUARE BEFORE DAWN

I opened my eyes after a short sleep; a light still glowed dimly in the night lamp, and I looked around me overcome with deep boredom as if in a wilderness. Where was I? And who was this man? I crept out of bed and dressed silently. Was he asleep – or was he pretending to be asleep? The door was unlocked and I stole away down the stairs with my case in my hand, and did not put on my shoes until I reached the outside door; and I walked into the empty street in the cold morning breeze, while the town still slept.

The street lights took the place of stars, except that they brought no message from the depths of the heavens; this was a world without depths, and I was alone – so alone that even that other persona of the self, the one which stirs shame and regret, had abandoned me; I was dull, and everything was flat: a person without context or, to be more exact, a woman without existence.

And then I was standing once again in the square where I had stood the previous evening; that is how the opening theme reappears at the end of a musical composition, only in a different key, in a different rhythm, with unrelated chords –

and with the contents in reverse; in reality I did not recognise
anything any more, except my wooden suitcase. The square
which yesterday had been thronged with busy people and
throbbing with many thousands of horsepower was now empty
and still. I seated myself on a bench in the middle of the square,
tired.

"What's wrong?"

"Nothing."

"Has anything happened?"

"No, nothing has happened."

In this way I took part in a long and no doubt significant
conversation, perhaps with some disembodied voice, perhaps
with one of those personae of the self or the godhead which
for so long has been lost, or has perhaps never even existed;
until I happened to look up and saw a man standing beside
me, studying me.

"I thought you were crying," he said.

"No, no," I replied. "I'm just a little tired; just finished a
journey."

"Well, well, good morning, how do you do?" said the man.
"Surely it's not you, here, is it?"

"Am I seeing right?" I said, for who should it be but my
good friend and fellow pupil of the previous winter, the unselfconscious policeman, that thickset man who always saw things
in the light of reality because he had such a heavy behind. And
I rose to my feet as is the custom among country women when
they greet a man and said, "And how do you do?"

"What are you doing here?" he asked.

"I've just arrived in town," I said. "From home."

"At this queer hour?"

"We had a breakdown," I replied. "It took them some time
to repair it. We didn't get here until just now. I'm waiting until
it's a rather more reasonable hour before going to wake people
up."

"Listen, dear," said the unselfconscious policeman. "We'll
have some coffee, of course, with our professor, he'll hardly

be in bed yet. And you can tell us how the music is doing in the north."

"Tell me about the south, rather," I said.

"Oh, my dear," he said, "what is a man to say nowadays? Child murders in the street are no longer news, nor even if men drink themselves stupid and insensible in order to raise the courage to beat their wives. The order of the day now is: sell the country, bury bones."

I said that the only thing I knew about that was that the gods had come north to us with two crates and claimed they contained bones; but that while our pastor was rounding up a cortège, the Government had sent for the crates.

"These wretched gods," said the unselfconscious policeman. "It so happened that the bones arrived from Copenhagen on the very day on which the representatives of the Great Power were demanding an agreement; with the result that Parliament was up to the eyes in selling on that particular day, and had no time to hold a ceremony. The Prime Minister sent a chit down to the harbour and asked for the bones to be shoved into his warehouse at Snorredda until the meeting was over. In fact, that meeting lasted well into the night, because the Commies are against the dollar, and so they didn't manage to sell before nearly dawn. And in the meantime these devils grabbed their opportunity and stole the bones."

"So we have been sold?" I asked.

"Oh, yes, the sovereignty's gone, I suppose, that's all right. Reykjanes is going to be some special resting place for welfare missions going east and west."

"And who all said Yes?" I asked.

"You're surely not so childish as to need to ask that?" he said. "Naturally all the fatherland-hurrah chaps said Yes."

"The ones who swore on their mothers?" I asked.

"D'you imagine anyone else would want to sell our country?" he said.

"And the people?" I asked.

"Naturally they ordered us in the police force to prepare

the tear-gas and other titbits for the people," he said. "But the people did nothing. The people are children. They are taught that criminals live in Skólavörðustígur* and not Austurvöllur. Their faith in this wavers a bit, perhaps, from time to time, but when politicians have sworn often enough and hurrahed for long enough, they begin to believe it again. People don't have the imagination to understand politicians. People are too innocent."

"Yes, I suppose I knew well enough the way things were going when they began to swear oaths up north in the summer," I said. "All trivial matters have ceased to take me by surprise. But since I have been so lucky as to meet a friend, I would like to ask you one thing: what news is there of – the Northern Trading Company?"

"You don't know that either?" he said.

"I know nothing," I said.

"Not even that he's up the road now?"

"Who is where?"

"Since you haven't heard anything," he said, "I doubt if I'm the right person to tell you the news."

"Up the road?" I went on asking. "What is up the road?"

"In Skólavörðustígur," he said.

"The prison?" I asked.

"We call it up the road," he said. "Up the road: where the small fry go. But all in good time, my dear; I believe things will improve. He got so far, in fact, as to buy the Cadillac off Pliers, his fellow parishioner. In actual fact he only blundered in one thing, despite the fact that the organist had often warned him about it, and us all: if you are going to commit a crime, you must first get yourself a millionaire, or else you are just a ludicrous person; and belong up the road; in Skólavörðustígur."

"And the company?" I asked.

"It never existed," he said. "And no merchandise, either. He never, indeed, actually claimed that the merchandise

*The street in which the old jail in Reykjavík stands.

existed, he merely said: the merchandise will arrive soon. And then he sold and sold everything imaginable, and accepted payment. But when at last he stood there with the money in his hands and was going to start importing the goods for his customers, Snorredda claimed priority for foreign currency. And the Government, which is one of Snorredda's assets, had come to the decision that petty young businessmen were for the axe."

"I can't understand what's gone wrong with my legs," I said, and took hold of his arm; truth to tell I had simultaneously a feeling of nausea and stars before my eyes, as if I were going to faint; and I asked him to halt for a moment, and dashed my free hand across my eyes to wipe away this plague.

"I shouldn't have started gossiping about this," he said.

"It doesn't matter," I said. "But I'm a little tired after the journey still."

After that we walked arm in arm across the road and behind the buildings; to the house; and I pulled myself together enough to be able to say: "Oh well, since we are a sold people in a sold country, I suppose nothing matters very much any more."

"Now we'll see what sort of mood our organist is in," said the unselfconscious policeman.

25

BEFORE AND AFTER ATOMIC WAR

Of course this favourite of fortune was in a good mood. He was working on his flowers, with sleeves rolled up to the elbow and earth on his hands, planting roses, thinning, snipping off withered leaves, weeding, preparing the ground for winter. Various plants were still well in bloom, including a few of the roses. But when one looked around, one saw that the house was emptier than ever before, the battered harmonium away, the picture gone from the wall. Apart from the flowers there was little left except the three-legged sofa which required such skill to sit on.

"Good morning," said the organist, fresh and cheery from his beloved daily work, his mere presence a peace-giving refuge, "and be welcome."

He wiped off the earth and offered me his warm hand, kissed me, bade me welcome to the south, flattered me and laughed at me – "Do please have a seat, the coffee will be ready in a twinkling."

We put my wooden suitcase under the legless corner of the sofa and sat down, and he laughed – at us for sitting on such a wretched sofa, and at himself for owning it.

"And where is Cleopatra?" I asked.

"Cleopatra took off when my mother died," he said. "She thought she might get a bad reputation off me. Cleopatra always had a petit-bourgeois streak in her, even though she was a great woman; and Napoleon the Great a great man."

"Napoleon the Great?" said the unselfconscious policeman in surprise.

"Fancy that, so you *can* open your mouth after all. How very solemn you are, my friend," said the organist.

"What is a man to say these days?" said the unselfconscious policeman. "The whole nation has lockjaw. As Ugla and I were just saying, people are so innocent that they cannot believe such a thing is possible; the man in the street hasn't got the intelligence to imagine anything like it. Just when we had finished fighting for seven hundred years!"

"Would it be impertinent to ask what you are talking about, my friend?" said the organist.

"Sell the country, bury bones," said the unselfconscious policeman. "What else?"

"What's all this, children?" said the organist. "Don't you want to have any heroes?"

"That'll be the day." said the unselfconscious policeman. "Heroes! Not half!"

"A man who risks everything for his cause, even his good name if his cause is defeated – I do not know who is a hero if not he," said the organist.

"Then Quisling was a hero," said the unselfconscious policeman, "for he knew right from the start both that he would be hanged and that the Norwegians would execrate him after his death."

"Goebbels murdered his six children and his wife before committing suicide, rather than yield to the east," said the organist. "It is a fallacy to think that heroism is in any way related to the cause being fought for. We Icelanders, who have the greatest heroic literature in the world, ought to know what a hero is; the Jómsvikings* are our men, they made obscene remarks while they were being beheaded. We do not doubt that in the Fascist armies there were proportionately as many heroes as in the Allied armies. The cause makes no difference to the heroism. For myself, I believe that the Icelandic nation has gained a few heroes in the last few days."

"And if their cause should conquer, are they still heroes in spite of that?" asked the unselfconscious policeman.

"They themselves know better than anyone that it never will. It has never yet happened that those who sell a country conquer. Only those who settle a country conquer. One simply must not confuse heroism, which is an absolute concept, with the fame of the conqueror. Take Hitler, the murderer of Europe: never once throughout all his murdering did it occur to him to surrender; he even got married with the noose round his neck. That brute Goering never cracked. Some think heroes

---

*A semi-legendary, highly exclusive band of vikings, who lived spartan and war-dedicated lives in the Baltic city of Jómsborg (thought to be Wolin, near the mouth of the River Oder in Poland) in the tenth century. They were wiped out in c. 990 in the battle at Hjörungavágr (now called Livaag) against Earl Håkon of Norway.

are some sort of idealists and kind-hearted people like you and me, but I tell you truly that if we incline to such an opinion it could mean that all those millions whom Hitler burned in his furnaces would be called by the name of heroes, or even those hundreds of millions of women and children who will be roasted by the nuclear bomb."

"But what if these heroes should succeed in murdering all Icelanders?" asked the unselfconscious policeman. "A military power is not long in converting a welfare station into a nuclear station, if need be."

"We know how things went for Hitler," said the organist. "People are immortal. It is impossible to wipe out mankind – in this geological epoch. It may well be that a sizeable portion of the earth's population will die in the war for a more expedient community pattern. It may well be that the cities of the world may have to be laid waste before this pattern is found. But when it is found, a new golden age will arise for mankind."

"That's small consolation for Iceland, if we are razed to the ground and annihilated by those who are fighting over the world," said the unselfconscious policeman.

"Iceland does not matter very much, when one looks at the total picture," said the organist. "Icelanders have not been in existence for more than, at the most, a thousand years, and we have been rather an insignificant nation; except that we wrote this heroic literature seven centuries ago. Many empires have been wiped out so utterly that we no longer even know their names, because they did not keep pace with evolution when Nature was seeking a more convenient pattern for herself. Nations are not very important on the whole, and indeed it is at one and the same time a recent and an obsolete phenomenon to think of nations as political entities: to confuse, in general, countries and politics. The Roman Empire was not a country but a particular armed civilisation. China has never been a country, but a particular moral civilisation. Christendom of the Middle Ages was not a country. Capitalism is not a country. Communism is not a country. East and West are not countries. Iceland is a country only in a geographical definition. The nuclear bomb wipes out cities but not geography; so Iceland will continue to exist."

"And you who are a man of culture – can you look with equanimity on them levelling all the world metropolises where culture resides?" asked the unselfconscious policeman.

"I have always heard that cities were the more valued the more ruins they had," said the organist, and laughed carelessly over the water which was beginning to boil in the kettle. "Long live Pompeii!"

"Yes, and do you perhaps want chickweed to grow on the pile of rubble where London fell in ruins, and duckweed on the pool where Paris sank?" said the unselfconscious policeman.

"Why not rose bushes?" said the organist. "And a swan on the lake? People reckon cities the more beautiful the larger the gardens in them, so that dwelling-houses can disappear between apple trees and rose bushes and mirror themselves in still lakes. The loveliest garden is nevertheless the countryside; that is the garden of gardens. When the nuclear bomb has razed the cities to the ground in this present world revolution because they have failed to keep pace with evolution, then the culture of the countryside will arise, and the earth will become the garden which it never was before except in dreams and poetry . . ."

"And we shall start believing in horses again," said the girl from the north, and lay down on the sofa behind her unselfconscious policeman, and fell asleep.

26

THE HOUSE OF WEALTH

It had long been broad daylight. My organist was cleaning up the room after all the earth work, in his shirtsleeves, with bucket and brush. I woke up under his winter overcoat.

"My goodness, how I have slept!" I said.

"You cheated yourself of your coffee," he said. "And now it is nearly mealtime."

"I'm absolutely amazed at myself," I said.

"Oh?" he said, and looked at me with a smile.

"Yes, to wake up like this in a strange place," I said.

"What is not a strange place?" he said. "We are all over-night lodgers in a strange place. But it is wonderful to have made this journey."

"Even though the world is a den of murderers?" I said.

"Yes," he replied, "even though the world is a den of murderers. What difference does that make?"

"And though the country is stolen from under our feet?" I asked.

"Yes," he replied, "even though the country is stolen from under our feet. Did you expect anything else?"

"I have milk in my breasts," I said.

"Go next door and do yourself up a little before we eat," he said.

He had been out buying food while I slept, all sorts of delicacies wrapped in paper, eggs in one packet, sausage in another, dried fish in a third, butter, curds, cream; and one larger parcel which I thought contained cheese. We sat on the kitchen table and dangled our legs and regaled ourselves on these delicacies out of the packets.

Finally I spoke up and said, "Well, tell me now, what has . . . my young man done?"

"In our society there is only one really dangerous crime," he said, "and that is to come from the country. That is why all the cities of the world will fall in ruins."

"But he had a vocation," I said. "He must have had something in mind."

"Yes, that is one of the greatest disasters which a country person can suffer," he said. "Take, for instance, the Maid of Orleans; all at once famous saints had started ordering the poor girl about while she was herding sheep."

"But still, she saved France," I said.

"That I do not believe," said the organist: "it is a fundamental misunderstanding. Historians have proved that the saints who did all the talking were characters out of fictitious supernatural stories from Constantinople; even God himself made a fool of the girl by letting her hear the voices of saints who, as none knew better than He, had never existed. Finally the wretched girl was burned – through a misunderstanding. There is nothing so dangerous for country people as to start listening to heavenly voices."

"Was he perhaps going to free the country," I asked.

"No, no, thank goodness, it wasn't as bad as all that," said the organist. "On the other hand he once heard a voice from heaven which said to him, when he was mowing hay: If you want to become a man, you must ride south at once and become a thief."

"To the best of my knowledge he came south to become a policeman," I said.

"In the *Edda* it says that every man should be medium wise but never too wise," said the organist. "He thought the best place to learn the techniques of housebreaking would be in the police force. Country people and saints, and even God, think that housebreakers make some profit out of it. I proved to him over and over again last winter that this was a fallacy, that housebreakers make much less out of it than dustmen."

"But the Northern Trading Company?" I asked.

"Yes, well, naturally an intelligent and musical person like him quickly realised that valuables are too well guarded for country people to get at them simply by climbing through a window at night. If someone wants to steal in a thieves' community, he must steal according to the laws; and he should preferably have taken part in making the laws himself. That is why I never tired of urging him to get into Parliament, get himself the backing of a millionaire, float a joint-stock company and get himself a new car – simultaneously, if possible. But he was too much of a peasant, and never fully understood me; and that is why it happened as it did. He thought it would be enough to float a dummy company like the Northern Trading Company and have dealings with a dummy millionaire like Pliers, and buy off him a car which had been stolen many times over; whereas it has to be genuine joint-stock company and a genuine millionaire and a new car of this year's make straight from the factory. In other words, he made blunders in all the technical details of his vocation. The obvious outcome is that he, who ought to have started by setting up house at Austurvöllur, is now resident in Skólavörðustígur."

"Is it possible to save a little fellow who has got on the wrong side of the law?" I asked.

"It is always difficult to save country people," said the organist. "Penal laws are passed to protect criminals and punish the others who are too naive to understand society. But though the nature of our friend's performance bordered on the most childish of crimes, like housebreaking, it has one redeeming feature, in that his methods were near enough to general business practice to make it debatable whether to convict him would not be an insult to some of our upper-class citizens. In actual fact he only needs a little less than 100,000 krónur to get free."

I pondered this for a while, but soon realised what a hopeless impossiblity this was: "My father and mother are now in their old age, and I am quite sure that even if all their life's earnings were added up they would not reach the sum you mentioned."

"Don't you think it right that such a man should be allowed to test the effect of his folly and obstinancy on his own body?" said the organist. "Can anything else save him?"

I had finished eating and was gazing out of the window at the withered weeds around the house, but at this question I turned towards him and said unthinkingly, "He is the father of little Guðrún, and whether he goes to prison or not he is my man."

"All right, dear," said the organist without laughing at me. "I did not know how you regarded the matter."

"I didn't know either – until now; today; particularly after the night which has just passed. But I don't have 100,000 krónur."

He smiled warily and looked at me distantly. "Búi Árland," he said, "your Member of Parliament and former employer, would soon write you out a cheque for that amount . . ."

"I prefer to wait for my man until he comes out," I said.

"Búi Árland is the best of fellows, we once went to school together; I know he would do it like a shot."

"Búi Árland is the dearest man in Iceland," I said. "Who should know that better than I, having slept with him last night?"

"Listen, dear," said the organist. "Should we not have some coffee to follow, anyway? There are some pastries in a bag here."

"I'll make it," I said. "You have done well already: bought food in many packets, prepared your flowers for the winter, and scrubbed out the house. But listen, where's the picture of our Skarpheðinn Njálsson with the cloven head, otherwise known as Cleopatra the Fair? How I miss her."

"I burned her," he said. "I am thinking of having a change of picture. A man has to do some stocktaking every now and again. And you, my dear?"

"I'm going to find myself a job and go to night-school," I

replied. "And when I've saved up some money I'm going to start learning in earnest to be a children's nurse."

We drank coffee and were satisfied.

"Well," I said. "Thank you very much. Now I'm going into town to look for something for myself."

"Go your road," he said. "And all the very best. And our friend in Skólavörðustígur – that is all settled, is it not?"

"Yes," I said. "That's all settled: he is my man."

This organist, whom people considered above gods, and gods above people, he who was in actual fact most remote from women and yet the only man where a woman could ultimately find refuge – before I knew it he clasped my head with his slender fingers, bent over it, and kissed my hair at the parting, right on the crown. Then he turned away and lifted from the kitchen table the parcel which we had not yet touched, and which I thought contained cheese. He unwrapped the paper with brisk movements. And it was crammed with bank-notes.

"Help yourself," he said.

"Is that real money?" I asked.

"Hardly," he said. "At least I did not manufacture it myself. But bring your case over here, just the same."

"How do you imagine I could ever think of accepting all this?" I said.

"Very well, then, my dear," he said. "Then we shall put it in the fire."

He walked with the pile of notes into the living room straight for the fire; I do not doubt that if he had had his way he would have thrust all this wealth into the fire right before my eyes, and then turned round to face me with a childish titter – and then never mentioned the matter again. But I ran to stop him, seized hold of his hands, and cried, "No, no, I'll accept it." Then he handed me the money.

"On one condition, though," he said as he placed the money in my hands: "that you never tell anyone where you got this money from, whether I am alive or dead."

And while I was struggling to cram all this money into my

suitcase, red in the face and bereft of speech and suffused all over with hot shame, did I not see him snipping all the loveliest blooms from his plants and arranging them into a bouquet!

"What are you doing to your flowers?" I said.

He tied the stalks together with fibre twine and handed me the bouquet with a smile.

"I know that no other bride in this country has ever been given a more beautiful bouquet," I said.

"I shall be content if you will look at them for me while they are alive and burn them for me when they are dead," he said. "And now goodbye, and thank you for coming. And give my good wishes to our friend."

A slim, slightly-built man; perhaps he was not in good health; when I embraced him and laid my face on his shoulder I felt him tremble a little.

But when he had seen me to the paving, and was turning to go back into the house, he suddenly remembered something and said apologetically, "Oh, I nearly forgot, don't come back here if you are looking for me again. I am moving today. I sold the house yesterday."

"Where are you going?" I asked.

"The same road as the flowers," he replied.

"And the flowers?" I said. "Who will look after them?"

"Flowers are immortal," he said, and laughed. "You cut them in autumn and they grow again in spring – somewhere."

27

IMMORTAL FLOWERS

When I was on my way to the prison in Skólavörðustígur with my case and my bouquet I happened to pass by the cathedral, and before I knew it I had blundered into the middle of a funeral; the coffin was just being carried out of church.

This was no small fry being buried, judging by all the ceremonial; as far as I could see it was the overlords of the country, whom I had learned to know by sight last year when I opened the door to them at night, who were now gathered again, dressed in black and white, with tile-hats in their hands: the Prime Minister and the other Ministers, the sheep-rot director, some Members of Parliament, wholesalers and judges, the mournful lead-grey man who published the paper, the bishops and the oil-processing plant director. This little group formed a circle round an exceedingly ornate coffin, which was carried by the pick of this *corps d'élite*, the Prime Minister leading on one side, and on the other side the mournful lead-grey man who published the paper; next came a handsome, virile man with grey-flecked hair and aquiline nose, horn-rimmed glasses like a mask, snowy-white gloves and a tile-hat in his free hand, quite at ease in this company. Who was he? Could it be true? Was I seeing right? Or was I still dreaming – one of those dreams of uncertain joy?

"All that you ask for, you shall have." Somehow I had never been able to place it until now, when an old Christian text which I had learned as a child flashed into my mind again: "All these things will I give thee, if thou wilt fall down . . ."

The strangest thing about this ultra-distinguished funeral was that there was no cortège behind the coffin; where now were the Youth Fellowships, the schools, the University Citizens' Association, the Road Sweepers' Association, the Women's Guilds, the Office Workers' Association, the Artists' Association, the Equestrian Association? No, no people, no bystanders, no mourners; even the solitary dog which in its time had followed a genius of the celestial heights did not consider itself worthy of sniffing along behind this funeral. Was it conceivable that someone had furtively managed to lift up the coffin lid? And seen what? Portuguese Sardines? Or even D.L. itself? And then taken the news straight to the populace? And if so, who? Surely not the Communists yet again?

Ordinary citizens went about their business in the street in complete indifference, without so much as a glance in the direction of this ceremony. But a few paces farther on stood a crowd of street-boys who were jeering at the tile-hats as they walked along beneath their burden. One could hear the atom poet's elegy being hummed:

> Óli the Figure is fallen,
> Eclipser of the people,
> The fell fiend of Keflavík;
> He wanted to sell the country,
> He wanted to dig up bones;
> Wet as a jellyfish
> He wanted atom war in Keflavík.
> Óli the Figure is fallen,
> Eclipser of our people,
> The fell fiend of Keflavík.

I looked around for the quickest way to escape from this square, pressed my bouquet closer to me, and took to my heels. What point would there have seemed to be in living if there had not been these flowers?